aNNA'S hELP

Jill Luebbering

Thanks for reading!

♡ Jill

To my husband, Jason, who encouraged me
to finish this story.

CONTENTS

1   gOODBYE   1

2   hEAVY   16

3   mESSAGES   33

4   tHIEF   58

5   iNFORMANT   61

6   cOUNSELOR   78

7   dECEMBER   93

8   fRIEND   120

9   eIGHTEEN   139

10 aPRIL   158

11 pROM   178

12 aFTER   195

13 sUMMER   206

14 gOODBYE   213

I never saw a moor,

I never saw the sea,

Yet know I how the heather looks,

And what a wave must be.

I never spoke with God,

Nor visited in heaven,

Yet certain am I of the spot

As if the chart were given.

Emily Dickinson

1 GOODBYE

"Good morning, Tiddlywinks."

I didn't have to open my eyes to know I was not in my room. Well, the room I *wanted* to still *be* my room. If I remained still, refusing to flutter my lashes, would she go away? Would today never have to continue? I could wake up next year maybe. If I went back to sleep, I could finish the wonderful dream I was enjoying before she broke my reverie with her greeting. The images seemed real. They were real. The colors proved it. I sat alone on the shore of the lake, my hands resting on rocky earth. The ever-changing smells drifting across the water. Yes, my dreams had smells, odd. I wanted to know who that stranger was approaching in my imagination. Why can't you tune back into a dream once you've awoken?

"Good morning, Tiddlywinks."

Again. Why? Why? *Why* did she insist on calling

me that juvenile nickname? Without opening my eyes, I spoke in a choked whisper. "Mom, my name is Anna. However, since I'm starting a new school, I'm changing it to Cheyenne." Knowing her response would be a chuckle, I opened one eye and peeked, while my second eye held tight to the last trace of my peaceful lake scene.

"Mothers name their children. Therefore, Mothers should have every right to nickname their children," she replied. "I happen to adore *Tiddlywinks*. It was your favorite game when you were three, and Grandma B. sat for hours playing it with you without complaint."

"It's moronic. And my new classmates will not hear it uttered from your lips." I had more strength now that I was fully conscious. Starting the day with an argument seemed fitting for today. "These kids don't know me. They don't need to be introduced to 'Tiddlywinks' the bizarre girl from Wyoming."

"Ok," she returned. "But how will it sound to introduce yourself as 'Cheyenne,' from Cheyenne?" Pulling my covers off in one swift motion left me not only cold, exposed, and irritated, but sad as well. She was right of course. (She always was.) I could not take on the name of my former residence. Leaving Wyoming for the state of Missouri had broken my spirit and seemed to have shifted my core existence.

"Fine." Pulling the covers back over my head and slamming my eyes shut, I decided right then my new school could wait one more day. They survived a quarter of the year without my attendance. What's one more day?

"I'll keep the name Anna, but I'm not going to school." Seconds passed, no reply. Victory! New plan for today, reread the Twilight Series. The gloomy setting of Forks, Washington matched my mood, and spending some time with Edward would distract me from reality.

"It takes seven minutes to drive to St. Mark. You need to leave in forty minutes," came her delayed answer to my rebuke. "So no, you cannot delay your fresh start. Lying around the house reading all day does not earn you a diploma."

Had she inherited Edward Cullen's unique gift of mind reading? Slowly removing myself from the queen mattress that recently replaced my twin we abandoned in Wyoming, I inched to a vertical position and planted two feet on the floor. One step forward and it was inevitable. Today would officially begin. Forty minutes to brush my hair, brush my teeth, put on a plaid skirt and white polo, and swallow a banana. Maybe I wouldn't even chew the banana. That was entirely too much energy being consumed in a short forty minutes. Not to mention the flight of stairs I had to descend to get to the kitchen.

After scrubbing the morning breath from my mouth and examining my grouchy reflection for several seconds, I couldn't help noticing the irony of what I saw in the mirror. My previous bathroom had walls painted gray. Here, my Mother insisted on having a cheerful, yellow bathroom. Fresh start. Hardly.

In the kitchen I found my banana, my Dad, and my Uncle Syd. The two were discussing plans for the new concrete plant being opened that would be their employment.

"It's too bad we can't transplant our loyal contractors to Missouri," Syd mumbled to my Dad, his mouth full of bagel. "We worked our butts off making them happy, now we are starting from scratch." Half listening to their conversation I had a flashback to the day my Dad came home with the "good news" of our move. The too-generous owners of the concrete plant Dad managed, the Fosters, offered him an unexpected, and impossible to pass up, opportunity. Apparently, there was room for another plant in Missouri, and the Foster family wanted to capitalize. Why would people choose *willingly* to build a home or business in Missouri? Got me.

"Anna, what did the fish say when he hit a concrete wall?" Syd had swallowed his bagel and was attempting a comedy routine. My answer was to turn my back and walk back upstairs to retrieve my backpack.

"Dam!" Syd hollered after my retreating back. Thank goodness he couldn't see me roll my eyes. I really did love him.

"What's her problem?" he asked in a hurt voice.

"Teenitis," came my Mother's voice, loud enough that she knew I could hear despite being at the top of the stairs. "In the infamous words of Grandma B., 'This too shall pass.'" Their words became more muffled as I headed back to my room for my bag. I slung my navy backpack over both shoulders remembering how I had observed most students at St. Mark High School carrying their bags when I toured the school three weeks ago. At my old school we carried our books. I guess in Missouri it made more sense to put them in a bag and lug the whole lot around all day. Another mystery.

"Anna!" My Dad's voice was warm floating up the stairs. Despite the stress he had been under the last twelve weeks, he remained the rock of our eccentric little family.

"Yeah, Dad, I'm coming back down." Putting a little more speed in my actions, I took the steps two at a time and landed with a solid pounce right in my Dad's arms.

"Nice dismount, thinking of joining an Olympic team for stair climbers?" he laughed, knowing my lack of athleticism. He hugged me tight and then held me at arm's length. "Can you give Syd a ride to the market on Elm Street? It's on your way to school." And then moving in close again he whispered in my ear, "He's planning to make his ultimate nachos for dinner tonight. Just for you." Guilt trip. I ignore Syd's lame joke; he makes my favorite dinner. My amazing Uncle Syd. Selfless, generous, humorous, fashionable, and lovable. I need to make it up to him. With more than a ride to the market.

"You bet, Dad. See you tonight. Good luck paving Missouri. Hope you have a productive day." My words were sincere. I did want my Dad to succeed here. Even though it was not the geographical position I would have chosen, trying to be happy and supportive for my Dad was important. Residing right outside the city of St. Louis had to be better than rural Missouri. Although

Missouri did seem to have hidden beauty in its rolling hills and heavenly sunrises and sunsets, I still craved Wyoming's horizon, our urban home in Cheyenne, and of course my friends.

"Thanks, Anna," and with one last squeeze he turned and hurried toward the garage.

And muttering for only myself to hear, I added, "Thank you for calling me Anna."

Driving Syd in my Jeep was normally a riot. Given that it was only seven minutes until I would be taking my first step in St. Mark, it was a somber drive. Looking me up and down while I drove Syd scoffed and smiled while trying to hide his face.

"What? My new uniform not meeting your fashion police standards today?" My question came out with more humor than I had heard in my own voice for quite a while. I adored Syd's fashion expertise on a regular basis. A definite perk of having a live-in gay uncle. His favorite hobby was dressing Mom and me. Wearing a school uniform automatically disqualified me from earning any high marks today.

"No, you look adorable in plaid. I was just noticing the pink in your cheeks knowing you don't have any makeup on. You have a healthy glow." Making me blush deeper pink I'm sure, I looked at him with a sideways smile and kept driving.

Stepping out of the Jeep into the school's full parking lot meant I was surrounded by dozens of onlookers. Secretly glad Syd was dropped off and not escorting me in, I walked quietly towards the main office. This was going to be a long day.

Sixteen exhausting hours later, my dream returned as soon as I closed my eyes. I was sitting barefoot on the edge of the lake when I heard the softest knocking. Pulling me from my sleepiness the knock was heard again. Confusion was instantly replaced with contentment as my eyes focused on my Mom entering my bedroom, closing the door noiselessly behind her. Sitting gingerly on the edge of my bed she reminded me of a picture we had posed for over a year ago. At the time we were dolled up for a night out thanks to Syd's skillful touch. The photo in my mind showed a happy and carefree mother arm in arm with me; the skittish but cheerful teenager. We were celebrating my sweet sixteen, my new black Jeep parked yards away, gassed up and ready to be the evening's chariot.

Tonight, my Mom wore similar clothes but much less attention to hair, makeup, and accessories. Still stunning despite her eighteen-hour workday.

"How was Day One?" Her question flooded my still sleep deprived brain with images of my first day at my new school.

"Tolerable," I mumbled. Honestly, it wasn't half as bad as expected. The teachers were predictable with introductions, revised syllabuses, and polite conversations. Lunch was edible, although I ate only a few bites. Hard to mess up a ham sandwich. There were so many students whose faces were a blur in the hallways, I doubt many noticed my unease when I walked head down to each class.

"The priest reminds me of Father Joel. Same friendly smile and talked too much. Apparently, this priest, Father Nicholas, is a huge baseball fan. Lucky, since Missouri has not one, but two professional teams." I recalled today's all school Mass. Sitting between two nameless girls who chatted across my lap for the thirty-minute duration, I remembered his words. "His homily was all baseball. He made some reference to having home field advantage and applied it to today's Gospel. Made total sense. Relevant too, if you understand the game." My Mom seemed to like that my first churchy experience was positive. It was because of her adoration for our faith that she insisted I attend a catholic school. I have not argued, and never would.

"Syd wants to dress you for Prom in May."

"Getting fancy for Prom would first require a date, Mom." Another flash memory of the photo. Me with makeup. I was not ugly. Certainly not billboard worthy, but I had a decent face. A splatter of annoying freckles across my auburn skin. Long, dark curls and green eyes, thanks to Grandma B., and high cheek bones. Prom though, was out of the question.

"Any cute boys?" Her question was typical. Always asking about the boys in my life. Probably hedging to make sure I wasn't planning to match Syd's lifestyle, not that she would disapprove too vocally.

"Not really. A boy named Josh, I think that was his name, helped me find my last class which he also happened to be in. American Literature. Then we walked to the parking lot after dismissal. He liked my Jeep." Josh, I'm sure that was his name. He looked like a Josh. Tall, lean, light brown hair and medium brown eyes. All smiles. Surely a boy this good looking would have a girlfriend. What had we been discussing? Maybe Emily Dickinson. Yes, it was a conversation about Dickinson living her life in seclusion. Today it would not be possible to live that way thanks to social media. A person would have to find a cave in remote Mongolia to avoid contact with others. I enjoy quiet time, but isolation would drive me mad instantly. That reminded me. I need to check on my friends back in Wyoming. See how they were surviving without me. Or at least remind them I do still in fact exist.

Mom gave me a soft nudge.

"That will give you something to talk about with him tomorrow: transportation. Maybe he drives a farm truck, and he's jealous."

"He looked like the farm type. Maybe he sells cows," I joked. Syd probably has a good joke I could start with tomorrow…Why did the cow drink coffee?" I did not have any intention of opening with a corny cow joke. Small talk with Mom felt good right now. Felt like home. In this non home.

"Good night, Tiddlywinks," she sang in a lullaby voice. Putting her warm hand on my forehead and leaning in to kiss my cheek, she looked into my eyes. "I love you."

"Mom. Seriously. I thought I made myself clear this morning. No more Tiddlywinks."

"What?" she mused. "Can I at least call you that at bedtime?" Her bright expression was fading quickly.

"Ok," I surrendered. "But only at bedtime." If even a breath of that putrid nickname entered St. Mark, I would be doomed to a high school career with no friends, no dates, and most definitely no Prom.

Kissing me one last time, she reminded me of her early morning meeting at the Health Department. No Mom at breakfast time. Looked like I would be having a banana again.

Day Two was maybe one fraction easier to deal with upon awakening. At least I knew what to expect. Getting dressed was always easy. Catholic school kids loved to complain about uniforms, but how nice, not to have to think about a wardrobe every single morning.

Taking the stairs one at a time today I made my way to the kitchen in time to see Syd's car disappear out the side window, and my Dad pouring himself the last of the coffee from the large pot. "Hey, Anna Banana!" he grinned as I grabbed a browning banana from the fruit plate. What was it with nicknames in this family?

Keeping my eye roll in check, I simply gave him my best glared smile and replied, "Just plain Anna will do, thank you very much."

"Right. Anna. It is a lovely name. Especially when paired with Marie and Cabel." His pride in my name was more than evident on his freshly shaven face. Marie had been his Mother's middle name, and her Mother's middle name, and her Mother's middle name, and so on dating back to when a boat out east hit the coast. I'm guessing at least. He had picked out Anna too, and enjoyed reminding me occasionally I was hand painted by him. I did look astonishingly much more like him than my Mom. Our eyes and expressions were "so readable" Mom always said. Again, with the mind reading.

"Off to the bank," he announced. Picking up his to go coffee mug, tablet sleeve, and jacket he winked, smiled and opened the garage door in farewell.

What is with the winking in this family? If it's not the Tiddly, it's the reality version. Peeling my ripened banana with too much force, I found myself looking at my breakfast as it hit the floor. Sighing deeply, I tossed it in the trash and settled for the box of mini wheats already on the table. As I counted my chews, I came to realize the peaceful silence of my new house was comforting and unnerving. I jumped as my cell phone vibrated and alerted me with a ping, I had a new text. Alexandra, I hoped. She never texted back last night when I asked her about that Kent guy in our (well hers now) calculus class. Oh, how I missed Wyoming. Deep breath. Missouri. Focus on Missouri.

My GPS says I've arrived at the health dept but I'm in front of a tractor supply business. I'm guessing this is not the right location for my meeting. Lol. Look on the kitchen counter for a piece of paper I scribbled an address on.

Mom. What would she do without me? She can't even use a GPS! This town is nothing but parallel and perpendicular streets. Glancing from counter to counter I spotted the paper and took a picture with my cell camera and texted it back.

Good luck not getting lost. And good luck at your meeting. Off to conquer day two. Love you :)

If she would focus on her GPS directions instead of singing along to the 90s Greatest Hits station she would do just fine.

Got your address pic. I went n instead of s. Why can't it just say left and right? Kick day two in the butt! See you tonight. xoxo

Oh, Mom. Please stop trying to be cool. You're getting kind of old to say butt. Ha! Maybe she read my mind that time! Grinning at my own personal joke, I grabbed my bag and keys and headed out to kick Day Two in the butt.

"Anna Cabel?" The voice was too serious. That should have been my first clue. Looking up into the eyes of the speaker I saw a level of concern I was not familiar with. "Can you come with me to the office please? There is someone here to see you." Too polite. Clue number two. I felt fifteen pairs of eyes staring at me as I exited the classroom. When you follow a stranger down a long hallway you suddenly become hyper aware of anything that involves your sensory system. There was a lot of dust on the floor. Electric pencil sharpeners were working overtime in two classrooms. The cafeteria was wafting unwanted fragrances of taco crunch mixed with cinnamon rolls into my overcrowded nostrils. My sweaty palms reminded me to follow the tall gentleman dressed in a suit Syd would approve of down the long, stuffy hallway. Were the walls getting closer as I walked? Was the floor tilting slightly to the south, or right, as Mom needed to be directed? The taste of bile was present as I scanned the audience I was placed in front of. How nice. A family reunion on my second day at St. Mark. So why the bile? My body knew something my brain did not.

Dad approached apprehensively. I know it only took two seconds for him to cross the floor to reach me, but still in hyper sensory mode, it seemed like minutes. His work shoes made a soft padded sound on the industrial office carpeting. His stride was weak, unlike the confident one I was familiar with. His smile was nonexistent. Were those tears? Eyes don't sweat, do they?

A hushed voice interrupted the ear ringing silence.

"Anna Marie." Funny, the voice of my father was not at all familiar. It was hoarse and sounded like gravel being churned into concrete in one of his fleet of six new trucks. "There's been an accident." More confusion. I know my ears were working because someone coughed, and I saw someone attach that cough to an open mouth and raised handkerchief. "Mom was in an accident, Anna. She is being treated at a hospital in St. Louis." I felt his grip on my shoulders now. Shaking, too tight for a school. What did he just say? Mom was going to St. Louis? I thought her meeting was at the Health Department. For the first time I notice Father Nicholas in the room. He wasn't smiling anymore. Turning to Syd whose eyes looked paralyzed with fright, I only then processed what my Dad said. Oh. Suddenly there were too many hands near me. Offering a tissue, a chair, a hug. I needed space to breathe. A tightness in my chest overpowered the pain in my throat. My brain was catching up to what my body prematurely knew. Bad news. Worse than bad. Unacceptable. This is not Missouri. This is misery.

Hours, maybe days later, I'm not sure, clocks are arbitrary objects when a person is in crisis mode, I found myself in a hospital staring at a clock on the wall. Batteries. Clocks need batteries. When the batteries die, clocks get new ones. Who changes them? There must be over a billion or so clocks in the world. It's not fair when you stop and think about it. Clocks get new batteries. Clocks are immortal. Batteries are not. We are batteries. Wait, no. I was taught not to fear death. Death is part of life. Jesus died like a battery to save us. So, we could go to heaven with him. And be a clock. Immortal in heaven. No, that's not what I was taught.

Beeping distracted my battery mortality. Focusing again on my surroundings I vaguely notice I'm sitting in an extremely uncomfortable recliner parked at my Mom's side. Dad and Syd left their post at the door and the other side of Mom to find coffee. I was alone with the beeping. Until three nurses and a doctor appeared out of nowhere to assess the new noise. A quiet panic was present as soon as the doctor told one nurse to remove me, and the other nurse to move the crash cart closer.

Another slow-motion episode was ebbing its way into view. Cold nurse hands guided me through the door, down the hall, and to a private waiting area. Hospitals were such busy places, but my focus was on flecks of dust floating in the fluorescent lighting, and the number of tiles I crossed while approaching my new refuge. The ringing in my ears returned full force. Must be my body's way of not having to hear my Mom die.

2 HEAVY

Exactly as it should be, nothing like I would have expected. Funeral weather was supposed to be cloudy, gray, dreary. A poetic landscape to reflect the mood of everyone attending. Nope. Cloudless blue skies, gentle breeze from the southwest, mild temperatures. My Mom's favorite weather. Her funeral day, so it makes perfect sense. I wonder if you get to choose the weather for your funeral day when you enter Heaven. Maybe people want their loved ones to be miserable. Not my Mom. She would want us celebrating her life. All her humble perfection. I can't believe she's gone and I'm just now appreciating her goodness. My weakest memory, one I keep in the dustiest corners of my little brain, is of her reading to me. Poems were my favorite. I loved the way her voice was like a song as she read the lines. I cannot recite these poems, can't even remember a single phrase. The dusty memory is sitting in her lap, hearing her melodic timbre carry me to my pleasant dreams.

My dream last night was more colorful and sensual than ever. The familiar lake sparkled from the golden sunshine in my mind. Lush trees surround the water giving shelter to brilliant birds that do not exist on earth. And the stranger took one step closer to me before I woke with a jolt.

Listening to my heartbeat through my ears instead of Father Nicholas's funeral homily, I attempt to hear my Mom's voice. I can easily get a song stuck in my head and hear the artist's voice with clarity. However, I am unsuccessful at recalling the sound of my Mom. Maybe her laugh. I will try that. The last time I heard her give a full out belly laugh was about a week before we moved to Missouri. Syd was marching around our two-story home ranting about the availability of a partner in our home state of Wyoming. Mom's laughter filled the downstairs as she reminded him, we were no longer residents of the Equality State. We would now reside in the Show Me State. She hollered loud enough for our neighbors to hear, "Show Me some men for Syd!" I even giggled upstairs when I heard Syd's reply of, "Eleanora Cabel! You are making promises I hope you can back up!" And then laughter. A song. The sound of an instrument more beautiful than a harp. More exquisite and more rich than dark chocolate. Fitting for an angel. My angel.

Father Nicholas's Gregorian chant broke the trill of Mom's laughter in my mind. The funeral mass was almost complete. Then it would be official. Mom was no longer a Show Me State resident. She was in God's choir of angels. Laughing I hoped. Surrounded by other gorgeous cherubs, basking in the brightness of eternal life. I guess my Mom is a clock.

Tears spilled at long last when I was safe at home, tucked into my bed. Mom gave me fresh sheets just Monday. It was Friday. I would never wash these sheets. Her invisible handprints were all over them. They were a perpetual hug from my angel. I drained my face of so many salty tears, my bedside would need a snow shovel to plow through all the tissues. More memories filled the space between my ringing ears. Mom and I going to get froyo and not telling Dad or Syd. Mom and I shopping for hours while sipping lattes, only to return home with shampoo and detergent. Mom and I walking our neighborhood in Wyoming, admiring houses we couldn't afford, and returning happily to the warm, delicious aromas of our little home. Mom and I pretending to watch chic flicks just so we could munch popcorn and judge the bad acting. Mom and I discussing my future: college, journalism, hopefully a husband. Mom and I collecting recipes that we knew we'd never create. It was just a fun mouthwatering waste of time. Maybe tomorrow I would try out that chicken parmesan zucchini boat recipe I pinned to my Yummy Stuff board on Pinterest. No, food was still unwelcomed in my new, motherless body. Maybe next week. Today I would master breathing without my Mom. Tomorrow I need to focus on Dad. He was an alien now. His lifeless body was unconnected to anything earthly. I better pay attention to his needs, or I will be an orphan. Can you die of shock at such a young age? My Dad was only forty-two. Although the last few months aged him tremendously. This week added another half decade. I fell asleep from exhaustion with thoughts of my Dad. He starred in my dream as a result. He sat with me by the lake. The water and trees were still. Instead of a stranger approaching, it was a gloriously smiling angel.

Saturday inched by, snail like. The ticking of the clock was a reminder to keep taking breaths. I should change the batteries. Wouldn't the ticking speed up? If time moved faster this empty, but surprisingly very heavy feeling would ease slightly. Or move to somewhere other than my heart and brain. I could carry the pain in my feet much easier. Feet were designed to carry heavy loads.

Opening the fridge for the first time I realized how generous our new neighbors had been last week. Obviously, I wasn't the only one who had no appetite. Half a dozen untouched casseroles were stacked, along with pies, fruit plates, veggie trays, salads, and cold cuts. Who ate when their mother died? As I began tossing food I knew would never be consumed, Dad dragged himself into a chair at the kitchen table.

"Do you know how to start coffee, Anna?" were his zombie words. His unkept hair and unshaven face added another couple of years. Guilt colored my cheeks. I don't think Dad and I had had even one conversation since Thursday. Unless my dream counted. That was a magnificent conversation, complete with his angelic wife.

"Sure, Dad." I deliberately made large, obvious movements, showcasing the whereabouts of the coffeepot and grounds. As my exaggerated movements spilled water across the counter, I thought I saw a shadow of a smile. Mission accomplished. Dezombie Dad: Phase one is a success. He is capable of smiling. Phase two, consumption. As I poured hot coffee in his favorite mug, I also presented him with toast and butter. Would he eat?

Coffee in hand he took a reluctant sip. To his obvious surprise, his daughter did know how to make coffee.

"Try a bite of toast, Dad." My concern was written on my face. He obliged with a small bite. Also surprised at my toasting skills. It's hard to mess up toast. "So, toast is edible." I gingerly chose my words. Monitoring his reaction with my newly acquired emotional radar. I had to keep this man intact. "How about some froyo for lunch?" A raised eyebrow and temporary lapse in chewing confirmed my assumption.

Swallowing first, he replied hesitantly," What's froyo?"

Pleased that he was taking bite number two, I replied in a voice that would not make him feel like a senior citizen for not knowing.

"Frozen Yogurt. Froyo we call it, another nickname." My thoughts immediately wrenched with anguish at my inability to allow my Mom to call me by a silly nickname.

"Oh." His only response. Then added after his third and final bite, "Sounds girly." And then with a chuckle that erased two years away, "Why don't you invite Syd?"

Ok, no froyo date. I get it. At least he put some food in his belly. Disappointment hung on my face though. And when I looked at my Dad again, he was shaking. Subtly at first. Just his fingertips. Then his hands shook, making him rest his mug on the table rather than take the intended sip. The shaking missed nothing. Working its way stealthily up both arms to his already tense shoulders. Oh no, I thought. What do I do? What do I say? Would my life now be warped with a constant question? Would I be able to survive and resuscitate Dad every time he had a breakdown? As I witnessed the first two seconds of this breakdown my mind raced in too many directions. Stay calm. Run for help. Dial 911. Find Syd. Just hug him won the battle. When my body finally caught up with my brain's decision, I found myself hurling towards him with two arms wrapped tight around his chest.

"Breathe, Dad," I begged. Salty tears made their return. I embraced him so fiercely I could feel our heartbeats in a symphony's percussion, trying to outperform the woodwinds, brass, and string sections combined. A minute or two passed. Possibly twenty. There were no ticking clocks to count the agonizing seconds until both hearts slowed to a steady pace.

"I don't know how we're going to survive this, but Mom would want us to at least try," was my attempt to revive humanity in our kitchen.

Syd walked in through the garage door just then to witness our teary tribute. The shaking had ceased, and the percussion had died out. What he took in must have looked completely normal for a father and daughter who had just buried their Mother and wife.

"Can I get in on that action?" Syd never failed at lightening the mood in any situation. Why would I think this would be any different?

Our hug became a huddle, and a few more tears fell.

"Anna and I are going out for froyo for lunch. Care to join us?" Baby step. I like it. Victory number two.

Syd's charming smile flashed as his eyes lit with interest.

"Absolutely! Eleanora and I had a local spot pegged for excellent froyo, but didn't..." Dad's quick intake of breath triggered Syd's midsentence halt. The millisecond it took to see the change in Syd's expression and my Dad's head fall into his palms was long enough to pull all three of us back into our huddle. More tears. More percussion.

"Let's go get some froyo," my Dad whispered exactly eighty-one seconds later. Without a clock, I can still count seconds fairly accurately.

Monday morning greeted me with heavy gray clouds threatening to dump an abundant amount of precipitation. Staying in my warm, dry bed seemed an acceptable choice. School could wait. Besides, my brain wasn't operating normally. Would it again?

Two downpours later my stomach growled. Tugging my blanket along with me, I found myself in the kitchen blindly searching the pantry for something that would cure the growl without leaving me nauseated. With a box of mini wheats in hand I turned to find myself face to face with Dad. A week ago, I would have screamed, jumped, and felt an acceleration in my heartbeat. That was last week. My body was in a new mode. Anna 2.0. In the fraction of a second, I absorbed the fact I was not alone in the kitchen, rather joined by the zombie-ghost of my father, I analyzed his morning. Yesterday's clothes, five-day stubble, red eyes, and maybe another two years aged. His greeting was to blink.

"Hi." That was all my mind could produce at the moment. Maybe cereal would kick start my vocabulary. "Coffee?" I said, pleased with the additional word.

"Coffee would be nice," he said. Taking his usual place at the kitchen table he sat staring at Mom's empty chair.

"Are you working today? I may have neglected to make it to school. I hope that's ok." Surprised by the flow of thoughts becoming vocal, I focused on coffee grounds.

"The Fosters know I need time. They're very understanding, and thankfully, patient." He looked away from the chair to the window. The heavy clouds were becoming a shade lighter, nothing was falling from them. "Syd offered to take some calls this morning so I could sleep in. I'm glad you did the same. "

Finding courage from the depths of my existence, somewhere in my feet I think where I was still storing the worst of the pain, I spoke slowly to my widowed father, "So much has changed in less than a month. The move, your job, my new school, and now, losing…" I couldn't finish the sentence. Turning to the coffee maker to hide my expression and work past the pain in my throat, I rerouted my train of thought. "We are different. We are new. We have to learn how to function and exist without our favorite lady." I did it! Speaking without tears. I had to be the rock of the family now. To hold us together.

"You inherited your mother's grace and maturity, Anna. I'm lucky you are here. I hope I can still be a father to you. This pain is unbearable. It hurts to breathe, to think, to sleep, to exist." His words were poetic in the saddest monologue of all time.

Sitting across from him I took a long minute to respond.

"Me too."

Tuesday ushered in with more clouds, but these were white. The smell of something delicious was tickling my nose. Checking my cell phone that was wedged under my pillow for the time, I was amazed it was only seven. I had time to get ready and actually be on time for school. School would be a distraction.

Fully dressed, and my long curls in order, I went downstairs to investigate the yummy smell. Syd was making crepes.

"Bonjour, Anna," smiled my Uncle. "You are in need of a decent meal before you attend school today."

"Did Dad eat?" was my greeting. Then added quickly, "Looks yummy. Do we have whipped cream?"

Syd produced a can of aerosol whipped cream from the fridge and put it at my place on the table.

"Not exactly five-star dining, but it's edible. And

offers enough sugar to get you through the day." Syd's cooking skills were typically amazing. Our lack of grocery shopping meant the only items in the fridge were the week-old casseroles and condiments. Finding ingredients for crepes was probably a stretch.

"Well they smell delicious," I offered. "Can you squirt a smiley face on mine?"

"We aim to please," he obliged. Picking up the can he squirted whipped cream to look like a winking emoji on my crepe. It turned out looking more like a banana peel. "Your dad was at the table when I came down this morning. He had an empty mug parked in front of him and was staring at the coffeepot. I offered to make him a fresh pot, but he shook his head, stood up, and walked back to his room. "

"Has he shaved yet?" My question was filled with more meaning that Syd easily picked up on.

Syd fixed himself a plate and filled a cup of coffee. Neither one of us began eating.

"No," he eventually replied. "I don't expect he will until he decides working is necessary. I'm sure this is all very normal in the grieving process. Shaving is too normal of an activity." And also, too final I thought silently. Of course, he wouldn't want to shave. The last clean shave he'd had was the morning Mom left for the meeting. The meeting she didn't arrive at safely. The morning we texted about GPS directions. The morning she last hugged me.

"So, we'll just continue this zombie existence until we all die, I guess." I poked my crepe gently with the tines of my fork leaving rows of indentations in a neat pattern. Carefully avoiding the whipped cream.

Syd took a first bite and chewed so slowly I momentarily thought I was experiencing slow motion mode again.

He finally swallowed and said in normal cadence, "Zombie or not, we're here, and we do in fact continue to exist." Chewing a second bite more normally he added, "My favorite sister in law is enjoying paradise. She does not want us to be miserable enduring her absence. I believe we can eventually achieve a balance of grief, life, and happiness. Just maybe not today."

I stopped stabbing and put a forkful of crepe in my mouth. It betrayed me by proving food still had flavor. Its sweetness encouraged me to eat more. In exactly seven bites I had eaten the whole crepe. Syd read my mind and refilled my plate with two more crepes. Complete with smiley cream faces.

After the second plate was empty, I asked, "Should we give Dad some chores if he's not going to work again today?" I started washing our breakfast dishes and waited for his response.

"That seems reasonable." Syd got up from the table and volunteered to finish cleaning by taking the sponge away from me. "Why don't you go check on him?" His guilty smile revealed beautifully straight white teeth.

"Sure. What needs to be done around here? I need to present him with a task that requires minimal brain activity, and no obvious triggers." Keeping him busy would be better than hiding in their…his room.

"Raking leaves." Syd's answer came quickly. "Your parents never spent time together in our new yard, and those damn trees dropped hours of work. Tell him I put a rake on the front porch. I am leaving to go sign some documents at the plant and go grocery shopping. See you after school, Anna." Another smile with straight white teeth. That gave me the confidence I needed.

I knocked as I entered my Dad's room. It smelled like his cologne which was odd because I was sure he hadn't sprayed any all week.

"Dad, I'm going to try school today. Can you try raking?" It must have sounded like I was talking to a toddler. I half expected to hear my Dad whine, and say raking was boring and hard and he didn't want to rake.

Instead, he lifted his head off his pillow and said, "School?" His voice was hollow and rang with concern. Did he think I was a horrible daughter for trying to go back to school so soon? Did he want me to stay home and hide in my bed too?

"Well, I was thinking school might be a good distraction." I stood without breathing until he finally spoke.

"Ok. I will try raking in that case." Exhale. That was easier than expected.

"Syd put a rake on the porch. I'll be home right after school. Love you, Dad." I closed the door without trying to be quiet in attempt of further waking him.

A Catholic school had to be the best place to return to after experiencing a tragedy. These students and teachers did not know me. However, I was greeted with polite smiles, quiet condolences, and a calm friendliness from everyone I passed. Principal Justice found me within the first ten minutes after my arrival to express gratitude for returning, prayers for healing, and a promise that my teachers would allow plenty of time to get acclimated. It was truly a gift to have this network of strangers silently supporting me through what was obviously the worst month of my seventeen-year existence.

During sixth hour I discovered that interesting boy's name was Josh. He smiled at me like we'd been friends since kindergarten. When I sat down, he immediately asked if I would like him to text photos of the notes I had missed during my absence.

"That would be great," my nervous, foreign sounding voice answered. Smiling enough to sound friendly, I added, "I guess you will need my number to do that. Can I trust you?"

"My last name is Justice. As in "Principal Justice." His smile revealed a smile to match Syd's. "I could get a written note signed by my Dad that I'm trustworthy."

When I didn't respond to that he added, "Or you can

decide for yourself."

"No." Breathe Anna. "I mean ok." Why does my voice sound so detached from my brain? "I can just send you a quick message right now, and you can save my number. What is your number?" Josh took my phone and tapped in his number. He let it connect before ending the call.

"There you go. Save me as Josh. Spelled J, O, S, H. It's a tricky one." Bigger smile. I wonder if he had braces when he was younger.

"Thanks," was all my brain could come up with.

Pulling into our driveway at a quarter after three revealed my Dad at least got out of bed this morning. Two small piles of leaves were surrounded by a sea of scattered leaves, and more still falling. Progress. I wonder if he shaved.

The house was quiet and seemed to be vacant. I took my heavy backpack upstairs to my room and sat on my bed to check my phone. Besides Josh, I had accepted three other classmates' requests for exchanging cell numbers.

No messages. Then, as if my phone was waiting to be held, I felt the vibration at the same instant I heard the ping. A new message from Carrie.

Hey Anna! Trisha and jen from trig are meeting me at the froyo place on high st to work on our assignment. Wanna join? 330

I should go. More distractions. Froyo probably still has flavor too.

Thanks for the invite! I need help with trig for sure. I will be there by 345

I put my bag over my shoulder and walked back downstairs. Grocery bags in the kitchen told me Syd would be making something for dinner. I peeked into Dad's room to find him sitting in a chair staring at a muted television.

"Dad?" my voice broke his reverie. "Do you want help raking after dinner?"

"That would be nice." He stood and walked over to switch on the light. "I started this morning but was interrupted by a delivery." From his dresser he lifted a large cardboard envelope. It had already been opened. He handed it to me and sat back down. "It's two tickets to the Bent concert. I didn't order or pay for them. I'm guessing they're my birthday present from your Mom." Knowing his love for this band, Bent, and how many times Mom and Dad had already seen them in concert, was hard to process and make sense of.

"Mom has, sorry, always had, an ability to pick out a perfect gift for her favs," I said.   Amazing. It made her seem closer than paradise. "I hope you go."

An hour and a half later I returned from the froyo outing with homework complete and two more cell numbers. The back kitchen door leading to the patio was open and smells from the grill traveled to my nose. Syd was grilling steak. That will give Dad energy.

"Hey, Anna!" Syd carried a platter of steaks into the kitchen and set them down next to other dishes he had also prepared. "I hope you're hungry!"

I dropped my keys and backpack by the door and silenced my phone. Sitting down at the kitchen table I answered Syd.

"Actually I am. I met some girls for froyo, but they'd already ordered when I arrived, and we got busy with our trig assignment, so I never ate. Do you need help?"

Syd put three plates on the table and smiled gently.

"The food is ready. Can you go find your Dad? I believe he's still in his room staring at the envelope."

I rose slowly. The concert tickets. Lord, help me find the words to help Dad see the tickets are a good thing.

"Dad?" I tapped my knuckles on his door and gave a little push. The television had volume now. He was watching the local news. No matter what state you lived in, local news anchors were all the same. Tight suits, too much make up, and cheerful voices even when the story was sad or horrific. Currently Ms. Reporter was warning viewers of a string of break ins occurring in St. Louis suburbs. Did I actually see a smile on her face?

I walked in front of the television and made eye

contact with Dad.

"Syd has steaks ready. Will you come fill a plate?" Hoping maybe if he sat in front of a steak, the aroma itself would encourage eating. "After we eat, I can help you rake. My homework is finished."

His glazed eyes refocused.

"The Bent concert is in December. I want you and Syd to use the tickets."

His hand clutched the envelope as if it were a newborn kitten. Parting with the package had obviously been on his mind all afternoon. He stood and stepped toward me as if not to wake the sleeping kitten. Extending his arms to transfer the envelope to my grasp took a minute rather that a second a normal exchange would have taken. After releasing it completely, Dad moved around me to exit his room and head to the kitchen. Syd's invitation broke the trance that had consumed my thoughts and posture, causing me to straighten my back.

"Food is hot, let's eat!"

Dad ate half a steak and raked two more miniature piles of leaves that evening.

3 MESSAGES

Being the owner of the Bent tickets, watching my Dad struggle to function as an adult, and the fact I had not shed a tear for twenty-four hours, nudged me to retreat to my own bedroom right after raking. Lying in bed would be therapeutic for my brain and body. Some of that pain was ebbing its way up from my feet. Creeping noiselessly through my veins.

A subtle ping resulted in my hand reaching for my phone without my brain even telling it to. Who was texting me this late? Maybe Alexandra. Oh, how I missed her late-night texts.

I would like to show you something after school tomorrow if you are available. This is j, o, s, h. In case you didn't save my #

My reply required some thought. Did he mean show me something at school? In his car? In his Dad's office?

Hey. Thank you for sharing your notes from class. What do you want to show me?

Josh seemed nice enough, but still a stranger. Just because his Dad was principal didn't...interrupted by a ping.

No questions. Trust me. I promise you will like it.

It was too late to come up with a clever reply.

I will think about it. Gnite.

I silenced my phone. I knew sleep would not come tonight even though I was tired. I was not ready to start late night conversations with a cute boy when other matters were pushing their way through my cerebellum.

Visions of my dream emerged. The image of that angel was vivid. My angel. My Mom. An angel. I wonder what she was doing. Do angels sleep? Clocks don't sleep. Looking at mine I read 10:34 pm. I thought I had gone to bed early. Running my hand under my pillow, I felt the smoothness of the envelope containing the concert tickets. A gift from my angel. Tears came then in torrents. The pain moved through my veins like cocaine in an addict. How could this powerful feeling not create any sound? My agonizing sobs racked my body. The emotions I had pushed down and evaded for over a week were surfacing effortlessly. Why had I held this in? For Dad? The finality of her absence was sinking in. No more holidays. No more birthdays. No more nights out. No more hugs. No more breathing. No more ticking.

Shattering glass interrupted my weeping. My head vaulted from the pillow. The weight of a sobbing mind weighed twice as much as a sleepy one. Holding my head erect was painful. Processing the sound required even more strength. To prevent collapsing back onto my pillow, I anchored an elbow and pushed upward. Holding steady and silent, I listened. Surely the sound was from downstairs. Though it had sounded so close, not muted from the floor below. Slowly lowering myself, resigned to my imagination playing tricks on me, I retreated back to my damp pillow and unwanted tears of misery.

Seventy-one breaths later more shattering glass, this time accompanied by a vibration. But I heard it more clearly this time. Not shattering glass. More like sweet natured chimes. But why a vibration? My hand automatically reached for my cell even though I knew it was silenced. Expecting to see the wallpaper I had saved from a screenshot Andra had sent, I was surprised to see a notification. There was no sender. Just an empty text box waiting to be swiped. Wiping my teary eyes for a clear look, I swiped right.

Hey, Tiddlywinks

What? I stared at the two words. How did someone know that nickname? Who knew that nickname? Why was there not a sender? It was a joke. Someone, but who, was trying to cheer me up? Make me laugh. This was not funny. Not tonight. I powered my phone off. I would rather wallow in my miserable tears than text someone cheerful. I reached for the charger and plugged my phone in. Adjusting my pillow to find a dry spot for my cheek to rest, I returned to tears. Morning would come soon enough.

Walking to class later than I would have liked only added to the dread of the school day. A night of little sleep, knowing I hadn't studied for upcoming quizzes, the random text, hugging only Dad this morning, all stood in line in my mind. Collapsing into an empty seat in first hour felt like an accomplishment. Survive the day. Breathe. Watch the clock.

By sixth hour I had at least an hour of homework to look forward to. Josh appeared at the door looking apprehensive, concerned maybe?

"Hey," he barely spoke audibly.

I guess he was put off by my abbreviated texts. He shouldn't expect more from a half stranger whose Mom was buried less than a week ago. "Hey," was my reply.

More volume with his next sentence gave me the assurance I needed. He wasn't mad. Just reluctant to approach me. It must have been beyond obvious my night was blanketed with grief. I bet my swollen eyes gave it away. "I really want to show you something. When you're ready for an outing. With me." His attempt to smile was pathetic.

I can do this. Have a conversation. "Can you tell me what you want to show me? Does it have to be a surprise?" My curiosity would have been an annoying string of questions a month ago. No way would I wait to see what a cute guy wanted to show me. Now. Now, I asked to be courteous. To show interest, even if it was fabricated. What could it be anyway? His truck? A song he'd heard that he thought would lift my spirits? Whatever it was could wait. I did not feel like playing show and tell. Even if he was good looking.

Josh's eyes crinkled into a genuine smile. "You just let me know if you'd like to be part of something life changing. I promise it will be worth your time." He opened his backpack and started removing his folder and tablet for class. Knowing I was staring at him, he turned again, facing me. "It can wait. Until you want a break from reality."

Throughout the next two weeks a routine was established. My Dad went to work when I left for school. Syd made dinner from a different European country for dinner each night, Josh gave me the same invitation every day during sixth hour, and an anonymous text tucked me in at 10:00. Never the same text, but always short. Only the first included the nickname Tiddlywinks.

Finally, my curiosity got the better of me. During class on a Friday, while the teacher was busy returning tests and answering students' questions, I leaned toward Josh and said softly, "Ok, I'm ready."

His smile revealed those straight teeth I had already admired, and sent a warmth through me, encouraging me to trust this guy even though I hardly knew him.

Josh met me at my Jeep at 3:05 as promised. The smile that he wore this afternoon was that of a child giddy with anticipation before opening birthday presents. "Do you want to follow me? Or you can ride in my truck." He pointed down the row of vehicles parked near me toward a shiny black truck parked crooked at the end.

"Well my Uncle Syd is cooking up something Swedish tonight, so I need to be home by 6:00. Where are we going? Do I need a passport?" Surprised by my own joke, I accompanied it with a smile.

"No passport." Josh dangled his own keys in front of me. "How about I drive, and return you here to your car by 5:30?" As he spoke, he started walking backwards toward his truck.

"Deal. But where are we going?" My confidence in his trustworthiness grew when I noticed a few familiar faces passing by smiling, nodding, or silently waving. Their support seemed to nudge me in his direction.

"Well, it's a short drive out of town down Highway 40." We walked to his truck as if we had been friends for years. Our steps were synchronized. Almost too comfortable. "I'm actually just taking you to my house." And before I could even put much thought into his revelation, he added, "And my Mom should be home by now, so you can meet her."

The twenty-minute drive seemed like three as we pulled into a long driveway marked with a red mailbox labeled, Justice. A song from the radio, *Simple*, by Florida Georgia Line, was now stuck in my mind as we hopped out of the truck. Humming only to myself I stepped down from his truck onto the cracked concrete. Before I had a chance to turn and close the door, Josh appeared Edward Cullen-like, and closed it for me. Grateful for his hospitality, I blushed.

"Josh, I didn't know you were bringing company

with you today." Her voice was deep, but friendly. Mrs. Justice stood on the painted front porch with a smile to match her son's.

"Hi," my confidence shrank a tad. However, Josh came to the rescue in a heartbeat.

He spoke to his Mom just as I would have expected. They obviously had a close relationship. "Mom, this is Anna Cabel. I have been begging her for weeks to come see what we have in the barn." A wink followed this statement that he absolutely knew I noticed. Barn? A clue to his mysterious show and tell.

"Ahhh," was Mrs. Justice's response to the wink. "In that case, I will let you lead the way." Her wave was not one of goodbye, rather permission to proceed to the barn.

Josh nodded, grinned, and turned. I followed him around the south side of the house. The stone walkway was neatly trimmed and surrounded with plants I did not recognize. I had noticed plants native to Wyoming were not necessarily common in Missouri.

We rounded the house and continued marching down the stone walkway toward the barn. Their backyard was more of a vast lawn. There was a wide-open grassy area sheltered by tall oaks around the perimeter. The absence of fallen leaves hinted at the care this space was given. Several painted picnic tables stood empty. I envisioned Justice family gatherings here.

I heard the surprise before I saw it. The tiny yelps

of a newborn litter of puppies was waiting beyond the large wooden doors.

"I was hoping you would agree to come two weeks ago and witness their birth but seeing them today is just as good." Josh's face lit up as he spoke, giving away his pride. "You do like puppies, right?"

My eagerness to see their little faces resulted in my walk becoming a jog. "Are you kidding? I have wanted a dog my whole life. My Dad was never interested, and my Mom said they were too much work." I saw the mother dog first. She laid comfortably on her side admiring her pups as they fed. The wiggling newborns all fighting their way to find dinner.

"Anna, this is Sadie. She is an incredible mama to her litter of five golden doodles." Josh looked at the puppies as he spoke to me. His love for these tiny creatures was evident not only in his words, but on his face as he stared down at them.

I stared too. What a tremendous sight. "So, they're two weeks old? "I asked quietly. Moving just as quietly, I lowered myself onto a stool that was inside the threshold of the barn door. Josh situated himself closer to the litter.

"Sixteen days." His voice was no louder than a whisper. I felt his volume was not to avoid disruption, but more in awe of their existence.

We sat in silence for most of an hour just staring. I took in my surroundings as well. This barn was not what I would have expected. There was no livestock, and the finished concrete floors were clean. It was more like an oversized doghouse mansion complete with glassed windows.

When they finished eating, Josh gingerly picked up one sandy colored puppy and nestled it into my lap. Sadie must have found me trustworthy because she had no reaction to my handling her baby. Feeling her warm body in my hands was breathtaking. Her miniature heartbeat was like a ticking stopwatch. A watch that kept on ticking.

"Thank you for inviting me today." Taking my eyes off the puppy I looked at Josh and smiled. He was stroking Sadie but studying me intently.

"We're glad you're here." He smiled too, and for just one tick, I felt normal.

I slept like a baby that night. A peaceful barn filled my dream and the sound of a puppy's whimper rang in my ears when I awoke.

I sent Josh a quick text when I finally left the comfort of my bed late that Saturday morning.

Need help dog-sitting? I am available.

His reply came within seconds.

Absolutely! Need to go to town anyway. Pick you up at noon?

An afternoon of puppy care sounded relaxing. Homework could wait until Sunday. Dad and Syd were probably busy at the plant. No one here would miss me.

See you soon.

Then without thinking I found myself chewing spoonfuls of cereal. Seated in the silent kitchen I was suddenly overwhelmed by the weight of my Mother's absence. What would she and I have been doing today if she were still here? Shopping no doubt. Our favorite hobby. Our house lacked much décor due to her departure coming so close to our moving into this new house. Maybe someday I would be in a mood to shop for curtains and rugs. Not today. Today was for puppies. To quell the heavy void of sound I turned the small kitchen television on.

"…string of robberies top today's local headlines," the news anchor was midsentence when I stopped channel surfing. The image on the screen was one I actually recognized from our suburb of St. Louis. A residential street close to the froyo spot warned me of the threat being close. I was pretty sure our new home had a security system but wanted to make sure. Reaching for my phone I sent my Dad a quick text.

Morning! What kind of security does our house have? And where are you?

That message must have confused him. His reply came so fast I had hardly set my phone down and taken my next bite of cereal.

I'm at the plant. What's wrong???

I should have been more meaningful in my questioning. Of course, he would be worried.

Chill dad. I'm fine. Watching the news. Robberies seem to be in our part of town. Just curious. Btw I'm going back to josh's to hold puppies.

Another quick reply.

Ok. Good. Had me nervous. We shopped security systems but never installed one. I will get syd on that asap. Have fun with puppies. Be home for dinner?

Typing a quick reply because I noticed it was close to noon all I sent back was

Yeah thanks xoxo.

The afternoon disappeared too quickly. Josh noticed I gravitated to the sandy colored pup more than the others. "I think you have a favorite." He reached for my furball, but I denied his outstretched hand by turning and instinctively guarding her small body.

"There's nothing wrong with playing favorites," I said playfully. "She feels my love."

"She certainly does," Josh smiled. "You seem content today. And very talkative," he added with a smirk.

"Are you accusing me of talking too much?" I was embarrassed. Maybe I babbled for these few hours and he was bored of me. I was sure he read the hurt in my eyes.

"No," he half laughed. "Just glad you're finally speaking. The first few weeks you attended school I wasn't sure we would get past one syllable greetings." The sincerity of his words and how he delivered them took my doubt away. My confidence slowly returned.

Thinking first, then replying, "Well, they say dogs can be therapeutic. Thank you for inviting me here. Again. Well I know I invited myself today, but, thank you." I was definitely babbling. Josh just grinned. I had a feeling we would remember and talk about this day years from now.

Syd was stir-frying something that made my mouth water upon entering the kitchen. "Hey. Can I help with anything?" I asked while grabbing a handful of carrot sticks from a veggie tray.

He turned and analyzed my appearance head to toe. "Yes, please change clothes. You look like a bum, and I'm concocting a feast from the Caribbean. And we're having company," he added with a huge smile stretched across his face.

"Company?" My plans for the evening included being as antisocial as possible and messaging my Wyoming friends' pictures of Missouri puppies. Who were we entertaining? Concrete suppliers? No, Syd would not be grinning ear to ear if it was work related.

"I met someone." He spit the words out like a cat

dropping a trophy mouse on the doorstep. I was supposed to be pleased with this new information.

"Where?" It sounded rude, but I wasn't sure this was the direction I wanted to see Syd taking just yet. What would Dad think?

Syd turned back to the stovetop. "Aisle nine. Ethnic seasonings and gluten free baking supplies. Marcus stopped and asked me if I knew where to find curry." I hadn't seen Syd act so childish since he was involved with Tyson back in Wyoming.

"So, he's coming for dinner and you only had one conversation with him? He could be the punk robbing all the houses in our neighborhood!" I gestured around with my arms like an actress onstage as I made this accusation.

Syd glanced over his shoulder and replied, "I met Marcus about two weeks ago. I've had lunch with him twice. I was bragging slightly about my culinary skills. He said prove it. So…I'm proving it." His profile gave away the smile stuck on his face. His cheek bones were too high. Ok. Syd is comforted by cooking and meeting men. I'm comforted by puppies. I guess that would make sense to a family counselor. If we had signed up for family counseling. Still, what would Dad say about this house guest? A quick text could easily answer that question.

Be prepared for a dinner guest. Syd is on the prowl.

Dad would understand. But would he approve?

I know. He told me. Think he felt obligated to keep me informed. Is there an emoji for how I feel about that?

I said a short prayer of thanksgiving. Syd's behavior might play a role in my Dad's sense of humor returning.

Three hours and probably three pounds of jerk chicken later I laid in bed satisfied with the events of the day. The heaviness of my heart and mind that awoke with me this morning, gave way to a day I wouldn't mind repeating. I wish I could talk to my Mom about Josh. And Syd. And Marcus. And Dad. And the puppies.

My phone began vibrating before I heard the shattering glass. Nothing was shattered. A notification popped onto my screen.

Hey, Tiddlywinks. Xoxo

I stared unblinking. There it was again. No sender. The high I seemed to be carrying from my day gave me courage. I should reply to this text. This person who kept bugging me with random messages wanted to be acknowledged. And that nickname still annoyed me.

Who is this?

I set my phone next to me on the pillow and looked away. A reply came before my head had completely turned.

Mom

There was a mistake. And a really big

coincidence. No one knew that nickname.

You have the wrong number.

Before setting my phone back down the reply came.

Anna, it's me. Mom. Don't be scared. Xoxo

This is not scary; this is a sick joke. Who would say these things to me? I had only given my contact info to a select group.

I could feel my heart rate increase and a lump rose in my throat. Emotions that I had neatly tucked away emerged with force. Tears exploded from my eyes and my energy drained. I felt weak, and I needed these messages to stop.

Leave me alone. My Mom died a month ago.

I powered off my phone and shoved it under my bed. Uncontrollable sobs took over. I wrapped myself as tight as possible under the covers and let the grief consume me.

Inevitably morning presented itself. My swollen eyes hesitated to open. It had to be close to seven. Light filtered through my blinds and offered a hint of the newness of another day. Another day without my Mom.

The house was quiet. Still uncertain of the exact time due to the fact my phone was still lodged under my bed, I peeked into my Dad's room to find him fully dressed and shaved sitting on the corner of his neatly made bed.

"Good morning," he offered without expression. He rose fluidly and stepped in my direction. The only sound in the house was that of his work shoes pressing into the pile of the rug. "How is Anna today? Your eyes do not look well rested."

I shrugged. "Is that your polite way of saying I look horrible?" Hoping he would not question me about my tearful night, I added for distraction, "Mind if I make pancakes from scratch?" Shadows under his eyes proved I wasn't the only one not sleeping. A hearty breakfast would benefit both of us.

"Ok, but I'm not sure you can top Syd in the kitchen." With that he turned and was out the door. I followed him with an optimistic smile creeping onto my face.

Twelve hours later I found myself hungry again, and Syd in the kitchen humming as he orchestrated our next meal.

"G'day, Mate," he accented in a skilled Australian voice. "How about a little roo from the barbie this evening? Seems we've eaten our way around the globe. Tonight's dining experience will include some fine dishes from the down under." He didn't look at me as he spoke. Too busy opening drawers, measuring, sifting, and checking his tablet for instructions. His busyness gave me a sense of security. He mastered every skill he attempted, and his success felt contagious.

"Smells really good. I'm ready for dinner. Need a hand with anything?" I lifted his tablet to check out what recipe blog he was using. As I scanned the list of ingredients in his Aussie Rissoles, a banner popped up. A message from Marcus.

What time should I arrive? I have wine.

I couldn't help myself. Teasing Syd came second nature. "Oooo, a dinner guest *again*?" My singsong voice brought his cooking to a halt. Only then I noticed how he was dressed; tight denim jeans, fitted grey long sleeve button up, untucked, perfectly messy hair. And barefoot.

A mischievous smile covered his stubbled face. "There is nothing wrong with inviting a friend over for a well-cooked meal. And Marcus worked today, I did not. He deserves to be fed."

Returning to his tasks, Syd picked up a platter of meat and walked out to the grill. As he walked, he continued talking to me, encouraging me to follow him outside. I grabbed my jacket from the back of the chair and made my way out the door.

Syd carefully placed the fillets on the heated grill, and with his back still turned spoke, "We want to go to the show tonight. Marcus has an old college friend with a minor role in some thriller that's at the Fox. He's had the tickets for months. He said he was going to skip it, but I convinced him to take me." An air of triumph in his voice he added, "He has four tickets. Maybe you could join us?"

I wasn't sure if that was an invitation or a question for Marcus to answer, but the thought of avoiding bedtime was a motivation to join them.

"I've heard of the Fox Theater from friends at school. I think I would like to go, and we are off from school tomorrow. That is, if Marcus is comfortable with a third wheel?"

From pancakes to the Fabulous Fox, this day ranked high on my "Life Without Mom" scale. Pulling into the driveway at midnight to an unlit house was all the reminder I needed. Mom always left our porch lights on. Even if we weren't expecting anyone. I tiptoed up the stairs, mindful to not wake my Dad. Eager to be horizontal, I skipped showering, changed, and brushed quickly. I knew sleep would come fast tonight. My mind and body were both tired, and I had had a pretty amazing day. I powered my phone off after sending a quick message to Josh, informing him I needed a puppy fix soon. Sliding my hand under my pillow I felt the envelope containing the concert tickets. Tomorrow I would offer Syd and Marcus the tickets. Surely Mom would approve of my charitable donation, they did take me to the Fox.

And then I heard and felt it. Impossible, because I powered my phone off. But there was no mistaking that sound of shattered glass and vibration of a text notification.

Hi there. Me again.

I had to be hallucinating. I waited. And stared at

my phone. It appeared again, accompanied with the sound and vibration. It sent an electric current through my body bringing sweat to my palms.

Who is this?

No sooner had I hit send, the reply was on my screen.

Mom

Immediate tears filled my eyes. I converted them to anger and typed two words.

Prove it.

Again, the reply came just after the message was sent.

You hate the nickname tiddlywinks, you were the last person I texted before the wreck, and there is a broken locket in your drawer with our picture in it.

Impossible. No one would know that. Except Mom.

Why are you texting me?

If this was my Mom, and not in fact a hallucination, there would have to be a reason. Everything happened for a reason. Well, except for Mom dying. There was no reason for that.

I want to help you, Anna.

I took my phone across the room and opened my

dresser drawer. Digging gingerly through layers of personal treasures, I located the locket. Opening it carefully because its hinge was loose, I saw a four-year-old Anna in the arms of an adoring young Mother. Two people who neither really existed anymore. I tucked my phone into the drawer but kept the locket in my grasp.

My reoccurring dream reinvented itself. This time the lake sparkled in moonlight and I sat with a puppy. No one else sat with me or appeared. I awoke more tired than when I had gone to sleep.

At noon I retrieved my phone, turned it on, and waited for missed texts to appear. Only one pinged on its arrival. Josh had messaged back earlier this morning, inviting me to come see the puppies anytime today. Just the therapy I needed. What a perfect way to make use of our Monday off from school.

Dressing in warm clothes suitable for a barn, but cute enough to hang out with Josh, I left home eager to put space between myself and my bedroom. Dad did not seem to mind my absence; he was busy on his laptop. Syd had left to run with Marcus and had yet to return. Knowing I would return in time to conquer a pile of homework, I promised to be gone just a couple of hours.

It had only been a few days since my last visit, but the little golden doodles had nearly doubled in size it seemed. Josh greeted me by putting my favorite little pup in my arms and smiling warmly. It was cold in the barn, so heat from the dogs was welcome.

"We will be finding homes for the puppies in the

next few weeks," Josh announced. "These two have already been spoken for." He nudged two matching brothers that were huddling together near their mother. My heart sank slightly at the thought of not being able to visit when they were placed in new homes. Sensing my displeasure, Josh added, "You can still hang out with Sadie. Or me." He was looking down so I couldn't read his eyes. His words were an invitation though. It was obvious now that the time I spent cuddling these pups was enjoyable, but I definitely liked the company I found in Josh as well. Our long conversations in the barn had filled a void.

"I would like that," I stammered. "I mean, thank you. I still want to spend time with Sadie, and you." I was rambling again. Josh made eye contact with me then and smiled broadly but said nothing. Instead he got to his feet and offered me a hand up, off the tiny stool I was situated on.

"Do you like coffee or hot chocolate?"

I returned the puppy to her mother's warm side and accepted Josh's outstretched hand.

Thinking of my Mom and swallowing a lump that had suddenly risen in my throat I asked, "Have you ever made a latte?"

"No, but I'm sure you can teach me if we have the right ingredients." He kept hold of my hand as we made our way in silence along the stone walkway.

A sunny Tuesday morning poured into my bedroom after a good night's sleep. My phone had been purposely left downstairs on a charger, out of earshot to my sleeping body. No dreams lingered in my mind either. A solid eight hours of sleep had reenergized my mind and mood. I dressed for school and headed to the kitchen for breakfast. Dad and Syd were at the kitchen table talking business. Both appeared ready for a day at the office. This had to be a first. All three of us presentable, alert, and willing to eat before noon.

"I will be back by nine tonight. I refuse to stay in a hotel. That would be a waste," Dad was mid-conversation with Syd when I entered the kitchen. "Good morning, Anna. I am traveling today, but my cell will be on if you need me."

I was not surprised by this announcement. Dad had often left town to sell concrete when we lived in Wyoming. This would be his first trip away since establishing himself in Missouri.

Choosing a box of cereal and taking a bowl from the cupboard, I sat with them at the table. "Ok. I'm sure I will be fine. Syd and I can handle dinner on our own." I turned to Syd, "What country are we tasting tonight?" Hoping Syd would take my challenge and prepare a feast, I was disappointed with his response.

"I am out too, Anna," he frowned. "It has been on the calendar for a month for me to go to the capitol building and meet with a few lobbyists. I am already packed. Leaving here soon, not back until Thursday." I could tell from the set of his eyes that he was not eager to

go. He put his mug down quietly and glanced at Dad.
Dad said nothing but looked at Syd and then back to me.

"No worries," I smiled. "I can eat junk food for
dinner, open your bottle of wine, and watch some R
movies."

My Dad's open mouth and wide eyes revealed my
smile did not give away my obvious lie. Syd laughed at
him and added," You should invite a bunch of friends
over, too, and smoke some cigars."

"Oh I get it, you're being facetious," he half
laughed, but then said, "Well, I am out of wine, have no
cigars in the house, and I will call the satellite company
and ask them to turn off the receiver." He stood then and
wrapped me in a hug. "I love you, Anna. Have fun
tonight. Alone. I will be home at ninish." Unwrapping
his arms from our embrace he walked out of the kitchen,
leaving me with Syd and the dirty dishes. I cleared theirs,
piling them in the sink. Returning to my cereal, I asked
Syd, "Why don't you want to travel?"

He looked at me with a serious stare. "Honestly?
This trip is irrelevant. No matter what I say to these fellas
at the capitol, it won't change their minds, or the
legislation they're brainlessly passing." His frustration
was evident in his tone and his mannerisms. Syd cared
too much about concrete. He was passionate about his
career, which was understandable, but sometimes I did
not grasp the emotional side of selling concrete. "It will
be fine, nothing for you to worry about." He too hugged
me and put a kiss on the crown of my head. "There's an
open bottle of wine in my room…stay out of it," were his

farewell words. I knew he trusted me to stay out of trouble. His warning was just humor.

Driving the route to school, I ticked off my day hour by hour. Class, class, class, lunch, class, class, class, chat with Josh, homework, dinner, homework, and finally a movie. Sounded productive and relaxing. The highlight would have to be finding Josh and asking about the puppies. Hopefully they wouldn't all be adopted this week. I had to visit them at least a couple more times.

As school days go, this one in particular seemed to drag on into the next year. Checking the time at least every four minutes, somehow, I survived through six torturous classes. Loading my backpack with almost every text from my locker, I jumped when I heard Josh's voice. "There she is," he was speaking to his father.

The taller version of Josh had the same hair, eyes, and nose. Principal Justice must have played basketball. His height caused me to fully tilt my head to address him properly. "Hello?" I said carefully, wondering why I was receiving a personal visit from the principal.

"Hello, Anna," he spoke softly, but with authority. "I haven't had a chance to talk to you for several days, just checking to see how things are going." His words were sincere, but somehow sounded generic. Like a neighbor checking on a senior citizen.

I was sure my reply would match. How can you put into words that when your Mom dies unexpectedly every fiber of your existence changes? Food tastes different, voices sound peculiar, even smells are off.

"Um, I am ok. Lots of homework tonight," my answer was worse than his question. "I really like spending time with your family's puppies," I attached this so he would know Josh and I had spent more time than he was aware of together in their barn.

His laughter at this instantly put color into Josh's cheeks. "Yes, Josh tells me you adore our newborns," his eyes were bright now, and he said, "Come anytime, Anna, I understand one pup in particular fancies you." He winked and walked away.

"So, he knows I like the little girl puppy?" I asked Josh when his Dad was down the hall out of range of my voice.

Even more pink, and looking at the floor, Josh hesitated to answer. Finally, he spoke, "He was referring to me." I stood processing this news briefly then just smiled, letting the idea spread a tiny bit of joy through my tepid veins.

4 THIEF

"Anthony!" his Mother yelled. He ignored her cry just to irritate her. Aaaaanthony!" she shrieked even louder. Why can't that wretched woman just get her lazy self up and find me? Anthony wondered. He bounded down the stairs in his boots causing the ceiling tiles in their little house to shake, knowing it would further infuriate her.

Sitting in the center of the worn sofa, his mother had a remote in one hand, cigarette in the other. "What, Mother?" Anthony barked.

"Why aren't you at work? I seen your truck's still here. What's wrong with you?" She put the remote down, but kept her lit cigarette in hand, taking a drag and exhaling in his direction.

"I quit," he informed her, knowing an interrogation would most likely follow this news.

"Why the hell for? We need your paycheck!" She struggled to get her heavy self up from the sofa but managed to stand and move toward him. Arguing with her about that pathetic job was not going to happen.

"I'm not working for that jerk. I'll get another

job. Landscaping is not my thing anyway." He stormed out of the living room assuming she wouldn't follow. He was right of course. His mother was so predictable. Probably already channel surfing. Anthony considered telling her he got fired, just to ruin her evening. Why would he want a job when he had other means for income? "And getting fired for being late," Anthony said out loud for no one to hear. Who cares what time the grass is mowed? He left the house, slamming the door for added drama. He didn't have anywhere to go, so he sat in his truck.

Sitting in silence gave him time to think. And plan. Mismatched batting gloves would do for tonight. The pair of gloves he wore last night were long gone. Probably a quarter of the way to the Gulf of Mexico in fact. No need to keep gloves too long. Two gigs per pair seemed sufficient. These gloves had been lucky enough in the past anyway. Anthony had worn these during the State Championship two years ago. He could still hear the amped crowd echoing in his mind, "Anthony! Anthony!" He wore these gloves to claim victory in a game which felt like a lifetime ago. Tonight, same gloves, new kind of victory. "Too bad no one's cheering for me this time," he muttered. Glad they still fit.

Success from last night's load was fueling his desire for darkness to descend on that classy, unsuspecting neighborhood. Two houses in particular fit the criteria. Unlit front, often vacant day or night, and inhabited by young females with pretty faces. Easily accessible from the backyard put one house at the top of his hitlist. Only forty-five minutes until nightfall. To waste time, he made a mental list of what he had accumulated so far on his little excursions: cash, game systems, jewelry, tablets, and a few beers. Tonight, he would focus on cash and jewelry. All pretty girls liked pretty things, he thought. Surely these two wouldn't let me down. Anthony was feeling lucky.

5 INFORMANT

Slamming my trig text shut and shoving it in my backpack felt amazing. Homework, check. I took more care into placing my tablet in its sleeve and sliding it securely in my bag between two books. With that task complete I was ready to relax with some food, a movie, and catching up on Wyoming gossip. I hadn't texted Alexandra for a few days. Wondering if she and Kent were still talking, I browsed our DVD collection. Dramas, thrillers, comedies, live concerts. I finally settled on Disney's Aladdin. I was in the mood for brainless and silly. I inserted the disc and left it to play trailers while I popped some popcorn. Dad would never think to ask what I made myself for dinner, but just in case, for his peace of mind, I ate some grapes and poured some chocolate milk. At least I had some nutrients mixed in with the popcorn and whatever candy I could find in the pantry.

Settling on the couch with snacks, a blanket, and my phone, I pushed play on the DVD, and started composing a text to my Wyoming group.

Miss you guys. What's new in wy? Ok here. I'm falling in love with a golden doodle.

Checking the time, and realizing the time change

three states away, I wondered what my friends were doing right now. Were they together? Alexandra's reply came first.

Miss you too. Wy is boring without you. I'm falling in love with a kent.

Her message made me smile. Even if they were having fun without me, they wouldn't rub it in. Whitney replied next, making me laugh out loud.

Get back here for a visit! I need a girlfriend who doesn't run off falling in love with wrestlers from math class

I could literally see Alexandra rolling her eyes. How I missed the sisterhood of girls I had! Our texts went on for the better part of an hour. They caught me up on who'd asked who to the next dance, which losers were smoking pot or juuling, and how a new hot teacher was hired for chemistry and he would also be coaching the girls' basketball team. All the news was meaningless, but I felt content just participating in the conversation. Like I hadn't left my home in Wyoming, and life was normal. Maybe my Mom even existed in this fantasy.

My phone pinged with a photo from Josh. He had put a pink bandana around my favorite puppy's neck. There was a message too.

Someone furry wanted to say hello.

I replied back a thank you and forwarded the photo to my girls in Wyoming. They would be interested in seeing the golden doodle I was falling in love with.

Then quite unexpectedly, instead of a ping of reply I was anticipating, my phone vibrated and made that odd sound of shattered glass. A message filled the screen that set my nerves on fire.

Where is your father, anna?!? Go upstairs and hide! There is someone outside!

I felt too heavy to move. Uncrossing my legs from under the blanket, I almost fell trying to untangle and stand without making noise. I did not take the time to respond. A feeling came over me that it was pertinent I follow these strange instructions. Taking the steps two at a time in the shadows of my house, I moved cat-like to the second floor. I retreated to my bedroom closet and sat timorously, hidden by darkness and piles of clothes. There was no sound around me which made my breathing and heartbeat uncomfortably thunderous. Turning my cell over in my sweaty palm, I switched it to mute and messaged Dad.

How soon will you be home? I'm kinda scared.

Not wanting to alarm him unnecessarily, I chose words he would not get too overexcited from when reading. How was I to know the warning I received was legit? Part of me was still frustrated from these random texts. And now I find myself hiding in laundry because of one of them?

As I considered moving, I heard it. The creak of door hinges that had been ignored far too long by neglectful homeowners. Directly below my refuge in the closet, the sound ceased, but only to be followed by slow moving boots across our tiled kitchen. I pictured a brawny man, armed with a handgun touching our possessions, looking for valuables.

No reply from Dad. I had to do something. My trembling fingers found the keypad to dial a phone number. I had to try twice before successfully typing the digits 9-1-1 correctly.

The dispatcher spoke purposefully, asking what type of emergency I was reporting. All I could say was, "Help, please. Send help."

Her calm voice betrayed my senses. I needed her to panic and yell to someone behind her, or into her radio to send police fast!

"What is your address?" I could hear her hands busy on a keyboard. "What is your name?"

Concentrating on supplying my Missouri address, and not my Wyoming address, I whispered, "606 Grande Avenue, my name is Anna. Anna Cabel. Please hurry. Someone is in my house." I was positive my voice was echoing through the entire house, I held my breath and waited for her to ask more questions that I did not want to be heard answering.

"Stay on the phone. I have radioed for help. They will arrive in four minutes." Her voice remained unchanged and lacked compassion. Did people go to school and get a degree in how to answer these calls? At least I did not have to speak again. She knew I was still on the line because my breathing hitched, and I began to cry.

My phone vibrated silently alerting me a message had arrived on top of the phone call. Looking down at the text I saw two words.

Don't move.

I sank into the corner of my closet and pulled a hoodie over my curled body. Praying silently that I would be able to hold my breath for three more minutes, I allowed my finger to end the call, not wanting the dispatcher's voice to be heard checking on me or asking more questions.

The boots were in my room. A crack under the door of my closet revealed a bright stream from a flashlight grazing around my room. Just as quickly as the boots entered, they retreated to the hallway.

I counted seconds. Ten, twenty, sixty. Sirens. I never thought sirens would sound like a symphony. Music to my ringing ears.

The intruder heard them too. His steady, quiet boots were now running through the hall and storming down the stairs. Directly below, I heard the backdoor open. He must have bolted, leaving it open.

Shouting came from somewhere. Everywhere maybe. Dozens of voices giving commands and taking charge. I wanted to straighten my limbs and get up to look out the window, but fear kept me still.

Dad's worried voice peaked above those of the

officers. I could tell from the timbre he was asking questions. Relief flooded my body. If Dad was conversing civilly, the threat of the intruder must be gone. Digging myself out, I cautiously emerged from hiding and crept across the room. Opening the door just enough to let the voices meet my ears, I was reluctant to go farther out of the safety of my bedroom.

"Mr. Cabel, can we please help you search your home for Anna?" an officer asked my father. It came across in more of a demand than a request. I heard doors opening and closing, several sets of heavy-set figures, and lights being turned on. Music in the background told me Aladdin was still on the television.

At least two sets of shoes were ascending the stairs, the first pair more hurried than the second.

"Anna? Anna!" my Dad was at the top of the stairs and now sounded scared. I swung my door open and ran the four steps to him. Not even enough time for him to open his arms for the embrace, I simply planted myself to his chest and exploded in a mess of tears and laughter. "Oh my God, you're ok! I love you, Anna!" He, too, began to sob. We stood there attached to each other for several minutes before he finally asked, "Why laughter?"

Feeling foolish because I knew our house was full of officers looking for evidence and listening with suspicious, or maybe just curious ears, all I could say was, "I don't know!" and I laughed some more. "I think I'm glad you're home, and I could come out of my closet, and I didn't have to hold my breath any longer."

66

Uncontrollable tears spilled over and ran in crooked streams down my cheeks.

We walked arm in arm down the stairs and settled ourselves on the couch where I had abandoned my blanket and popcorn. I picked up the remote and muted Jasmine's beautiful voice. I left the screen on. Something childish about the movie gave me a small sense of security.

Dad must have known an officer would want to ask questions, because he turned to a gentleman who appeared to be in charge of the crew wandering around our house and spoke confidently, "I am sure Anna is still shaken up a bit, probably will be for a few days, and I know she is tired. Can we take care of this quickly for her sake?"

The officer looked to be about my Dad's age. He was tall, broad shouldered, and gave the impression of being amiable just by his posture. He smiled genuinely and spoke as if he were engaging in conversation with a relative, "Absolutely, Mr. Cabel." He turned to me and offered his right hand for shaking. "Miss Cabel, my name is Sergeant Benjamin Adair. First of all, I need to say thank you." He sat back in the chair and placed a large heavy envelope on the table by my snacks. "Because you called 911 when you did, and our patrol had time to react, we were able to take into custody a felon who will now be charged with seventeen counts of larceny. We've been after him for several weeks. With your lead this evening, we got our man. So, thank you."

All I could mumble in return was, "I'm glad he's

been caught." Dad was right. I was tired. Leaning into his shoulder I closed my eyes and enjoyed the scent of his security. The two of them talked for quite a while. Maybe close to an hour. I dozed in and out of consciousness, and was pleasantly surprised when I next opened my eyes and found Syd beside me opposite Dad. Adjusting and stretching, I rearranged myself to move closer to my uncle. It sounded like Sergeant Adair was finishing his questions. Hopefully I could stretch out completely and enjoy some real sleep soon. The couch would be my bed tonight. The last thing I heard from their conversation was my Dad saying, "We're learning to survive without Eleanora."

Reliving the events of the night before may have been more exhausting than actually experiencing them. I retold the story a half dozen times before lunch, and couple more after I ate my banana. I certainly did not enjoy the attention, however, finding it a distraction from thinking about my Mom, her ostensible messages, and the last several weeks was healthy for my brain. At least this tale had a happy ending.

"So, you sat in your closet until the cops showed up?" Jen was the most curious with a long trail of continuous questions. Followed by avid listening.

"I buried myself under dirty clothes in the back corner of my closet. My muscles were so tense, but I didn't realize that much until I tried standing up." Really, I didn't notice my muscle fatigue until today when I woke up sore from my shoulders down. It had to be from tension. And my jaws hurt, too, from being clenched for an eternity. I was considering the idea of adding to my story one more detail about the footfalls I had heard but was interrupted by an announcement from the classroom intercom.

"Ms. Andrews, please send Anna Cabel to the office." The secretary's voice blanketed the classroom in a sudden heavy dread. Only bad news awaits when I am summoned to the office.

My teacher replied by looking at me and speaking abnormally loudly, "She's on her way," and nodded toward the classroom door.

I purposefully took a different path to the office than the one I walked the day I walked toward the news of my Mom's accident. I silently prayed my way to the glass doors separating me from more unacceptable tidings.

Relief issued itself into my limbs when I peered through the glass and saw it was a smiling Officer Adair waiting to greet me.

Holding the door open for my entrance, he extended his other hand for a firm shake and answered a question I had not heard, "Yes, Mrs. Beckon, the conference room will be fine. I only need to speak to Anna for a short time." He turned back to me and added, "Anna, do you mind leaving your class for a few minutes to speak to me?" He allowed the office door to independently close and ushered me toward a comfortable looking room with armchairs and a long table. I chose a seat facing the door, still half expecting my father to run in bearing the bad news.

Reassuringly, Officer Adair kept his smile on and left the conference room door wide open. He sat in another chair facing me with the same professional, yet friendly posture as the night before.

Noticing I had been holding my breath again, I exhaled quietly and spoke, "I don't mind getting away from class. Or my classmates." I looked at his chin as I talked. It was dimpled and gave him the appearance of sophistication.

Officer Adair's eyes crinkled as he grinned. "I would imagine your friends are pretty curious about the night you had. Hopefully they're not making you relive the horrible part and are focused on the fact you helped capture a criminal."

Doubting my own mental state for the justification of my fear level, I commented carefully, "Most victims would probably be a mess. Don't get me wrong, it was terrifying, I just..." An explanation was difficult to put into words. "My mind has been consumed with grief. Frustration, confusion, even guilt. It was almost a welcome emotion: fear. It allowed me to be me for an instant." Staring at my hands now as I spoke. I hoped the officer was not judging me. I did not want to seem like a stereotypical teenage girl who thrived on drama. I added quickly, "Last night's emotions pale in comparison to what I felt when I lost my Mom. I think I have been desensitized to other emotions." Looking up I saw an expression of concern on his face.

He spoke with confidence and compassion. I must be a textbook case, easy to evaluate and diagnose. "Anna, you are a strong individual. You are doing an amazing job of carrying on with the weight of loss, love for your father, adjusting to a new school, being a student, and now add the intruder. It takes a tremendous amount of maturity to balance that list." His grim face transitioned back to friendly. "Use some of that strength to ask for help when or if you ever need it. There are plenty of willing and able teachers, students, friends. Ready to help."

He shifted his attention then to a bag I had not noticed earlier. Shuffling through a manila envelope he eventually settled on a piece and extracted it, handing it to me reluctantly.

"Your father believes you are strong enough to see this and help us one more time." Officer Adair patiently waited for me to absorb the photograph he had handed me.

I studied the individual, assuming this was who they arrested last night and wanted me to identify. But I had not seen him. The photo revealed an average sized male, dark blonde hair, distinct cheek bones, and disturbed eyes. A stereotype formed in my mind. This creep had walked on my tile, climbed my stairs, and touched my possessions.

"You want me to say he was the intruder?" I asked, attempting to present myself as the mature person he believed me to be. I sat straight and maintained steady eye contact.

Officer Adair took too long to answer. Finally, after a deep breath, he replied, "We know this is the intruder. We also have enough evidence to prove he is responsible for the other break ins that I mentioned last night. We are confident you helped us accost the criminal we have been in pursuit of for weeks." Standing up fluidly and taking a few steps around the table, he turned and added with concern in his tone, "I want to ask if you have seen this individual somewhere before last night. Is he familiar to you at all?" He looked at the photograph as he spoke. "Because of the time of day, he chose to enter your home, and the fact your house was lit, we assume he knew you were there, and was looking for more than just valuables."

I told myself to quell the fear. I did not have room in my mind for it. It did not matter. He was incarcerated now. I was safe. Safe to forget this experience and focus on my more prominent loss.

"I still feel like a visitor here. The streets are unfamiliar, I get lost running errands, I rarely go anywhere besides school or the market. He is not familiar, but I cannot say I have never seen him. I don't know. Maybe I have." Tension clouded my mind. I could feel my muscles retract. Should I consider this conversation a portent? They had him in custody, why did I need to expend any worry on this matter?

"Anna, our goal is to keep you safe. Any information we collect now is bonus. We want this felon as far away from you as possible," Adair spoke with a severe tone and I understood that to mean he was working overtime on this case.

He returned the photograph to the envelope and met my stare with comforting eyes. "Have you met my twins, Allie and Zoe? They're sophomores here. They said they knew you," he smiled politely and waited for my reply. I searched my brain for matching girls with these names. I recalled a pair of twins in the cafeteria sitting near my usual table.

"I haven't really met them, but I'm pretty sure I know who they are." I hoped my words didn't make me sound conceited. I figured most students thought me to either be shy, stuck up, or a total mess. Underclassmen who did not have any classes with me, unfortunately, probably saw me as all three. "There are so many kids I haven't been able to really get to know yet. I bet they're great. And I bet they're proud to have an officer for a Dad?" I could hear myself rambling. My nervous habit was becoming embarrassing. My cheeks automatically brightened with color. Shut up, Anna, I told myself.

"Both of my girls described you as reserved," he reassured me without meaning to. "They know you're still overwhelmed with what you've faced in the short time you've been here." His kind words carried me through the afternoon.

I found myself at home thinking about the events that had taken place in the last twenty-four hours. In the last twenty-four days. Dragging my bag to the couch to start in on my literature assignment, I settled in for what I knew would be a long night of work. Good though. To keep my mind off intruders, and Mom, and cute boys who hadn't texted in what seemed like forever.

Right on cue, my phone dinged a new message.

Hey there. When do I get the details of your crazy night?
:)

Josh. Now he's a mind reader. Somehow I found this comforting.

Working on my lit homework now. Want to come experience my house? I'm sure my uncle will make something for dinner.

As I impatiently waited for his reply, I sent a quick message to Syd. Hopefully he was in fact making some amazing meal tonight.

Hi, favorite uncle! What's for dinner? Can I invite josh?
Xoxo

Syd instantly replied. His eagerness to meet Josh was too obvious.

Lasagna! I will be home in 30 min! What time is josh coming????

Still waiting for Josh's reply, I left Syd's question to wait and turned my attention to homework. Why would a teacher assign to write a letter to a loved one? How generic. What could we possibly learn from writing a fictitious letter? She probably assumed it will be therapeutic for me because she knows I will write to my Mom. Well too bad. I am going to write to Alexandra's Mom. Tell her thank you for letting me be her other favorite daughter when I used to camp out at their house night after night, eating my way through their pantry and keeping her up late listening to us girls laugh uncontrollably.

However, staring at a blank screen, I realized how challenging this task was going to be. Fortunately, a text from Josh distracted me.

Sounds interesting! Meeting your family makes me nervous. Should I wear a tie?

I literally laughed out loud. Surely, he was kidding.

Well if you want to make the impression you're from the 1800s feel free to wear a tie. We will all be in our usual attire for a wednesday night. Jeans. Lol

I hit send and before setting my phone down, I typed on more thought.

My favorite puppy is welcome to come too :)

The doorbell rang less than thirty minutes later. Josh beat Syd home. I hit Save As on my pathetic attempt of writing a letter to Alexandra's Mom and walked downstairs to answer the door.

Opening the door, I was greeted with lax Josh, thankfully not poseur. Dressed in worn denim and an untucked t-shirt, he walked in and handed me his phone.

"What is this for? Do I need to text your Mom to let her know you arrived safe?" I felt my eyebrows arch as

I looked him in the eye. My legs momentarily felt wobbly while I waited for his response. I held my breath momentarily as I let my gaze linger on his face.

A humored smile spread across his entire face while he hesitated with an answer.

"You wanted a puppy to escort me here. Unfortunately, none are quite ready to leave their mama." He swiped at his phone to reveal a photograph of my favorite canine. "Little furball was asleep anyway, so I didn't want to disturb her rest. I hope you are satisfied with the snapshot I took on my way out."

I looked at his screen to admire my little furry friend. Sure enough, she was the cutest of the lot. "So when will they leave their mother? Are you selling them?" Knowing how much these well-bred puppies must be worth I abruptly realized I did not even know if Josh's family were licensed breeders.

Josh took his phone gently out of my grasp and returned it to his back pocket. "Yes, we will sell them. It's my Mom's hobby. Honestly, they sell themselves. Hard to resist those golden doodle faces." His voice was laced with a sense of pride. Secretly I wondered if that was his future, his calling, a dog breeder. Josh obviously treasured these animals and it was evident raising them was a family affair.

Our conversation was brusquely interrupted by the arrival of Syd and Marcus, pulling into our driveway in a Corvette. Did I know Marcus was joining us tonight?

"By the way, did I mention my Uncle Syd is gay?" I smiled sheepishly at Josh who had his turn raising eyebrows. The grin attached to his expression comforted me immediately. I watched with trepidation as Syd and Marcus carried bags of fresh groceries from the trunk of the fancy black car, across the porch, and into the house. Josh was generous with offering to help but was turned down due to the fact that there were so few to carry. Syd introduced himself and Marcus, who to my surprise, hugged Josh with an armload of vegetables on either side.

Syd and Marcus disappeared through the front door leaving us alone again. I turned cautiously to Josh and asked, "Are you sure you want to subject yourself to this lunacy?"

"Absolutely," was his confident reply.

6 COUNSELOR

Finding myself horizontal a few hours later, I wanted more than anything to talk to Mom. I wanted her to know I had an adorable guy noticing me, Syd had an adorable guy noticing him, Dad was starting to notice he still existed, and how much I just really missed talking to her.

As if on cue, my phone vibrated and chimed a sweet sound I had not heard for a couple of days. The angelic sound cascaded through my skin giving me the sensation a warm breeze had penetrated into my bedroom. The sonority heightened my senses and I was suddenly wide awake. I reached for my phone anticipating a new banner message. Sure enough, there it was.

Hey there. Want to talk?

Never in my life have I been as sure of something as right then. This message was from my Mom. There is no reasonable explanation for why this could actually be happening, but it was. My doubt before of who was sending these messages ceased to exist. This was my Mom. I did not know how to reply.

Yes, I typed, not knowing where to start. A reply

appeared before I had even moved my finger away from the send button. Not humanly possible.

I understand a lot is going on. Fill me in on details.

A peace settled into my inner core and radiated to my extremities. I was texting my Mom.

I like josh. He's fun to hang out with. And syd has a nice boyfriend too. We all had dinner tonight. We laughed a lot. We talked about you.

My fingers could not text as fast as ideas popped into my mind that I wanted to share.

I bet syd impressed his friend with fancy cooking?

Mom knew Syd better than anyone. She used to say she could read him like a book. Of course, she knew he would use his culinary skills to win over a new love.

Syd has been feeding us well. I think my geography skills have improved learning about the foreign dishes he's prepared!

Tonight, we had dined on gyros and Greek salad. Syd hinted that a trip to Greece would be his ultimate getaway. I noticed Marcus took note.

Hopefully syd isn't overshadowing your new friendship with too much drama.

I laughed at that idea. Josh seemed to enjoy himself at dinner. He has twice as much confidence as most guys in our class.

I think josh was entertained by our family.

The logistics of this text conversation struck me suddenly. How was this even happening? Talking to my Mom felt so good, so natural. I loved, still love, her so much.

Mom can I ask some questions?

This time the reply returned after several seconds rather than instantly.

Anna my love is timeless. I am as much a part of our family now as I was when I existed. Your questions will be answered someday, but not now.

Her love is timeless. How ironic. The mother who became a clock in heaven is now sheltering me with her timeless love.

But is this real? Because it feels real. Or have I conjured your words up as some suppressed psychotic coping mechanism?

I imagined a winged angel, dressed in my Mom's favorite jeans and sweater, sitting comfortably on a squishy recliner resembling a cloud, texting me back while holding back laughter.

Its late. You have school in the morning. We will talk again soon. xoxo

The end of my week flew by in a whirlwind of

class, homework, another visit from Josh, and numerous late-night conversations with my Mom. This new routine became familiar and easy. When I realized Thanksgiving was the following week, I was almost disappointed knowing it would interrupt what I was finally feeling comfortable with.

I sat at our kitchen table pretending to do homework listening to Syd hum his way through the night's cooking when my Dad made an announcement.

"So, this will be our first holiday without Eleanora," he said looking at me. "New town, new house, no Mom," his voice trailed off. I knew he had something in mind that he could not put into words. "I was thinking how nice it would be if we could just go back to Wyoming and have everything back together, the way things were less than two months ago.

My heart sank at the reality of what had become of our family. What if we had not moved here? I would still have my Mom, my friends, my state.

"Life is messy I have learned," Dad continued, shifting his gaze now on the table. "I called the Shepards yesterday. They are more than willing to host us for Thanksgiving weekend," he looked back up to meet my surprised eyes. "How does it sound to spend four days with Alexandra?"

I literally felt my heart jolt with excitement. It seemed impossible to form a coherent response. My mouth produced no answer, instead I jumped from my chair and hugged my Dad. The embrace that he returned to me conveyed that this trip would be just as therapeutic for him as it would be for me. I let go after several seconds and turned to Syd.

"You'll come too, right?" I stared unblinkingly into my Uncle's green eyes. Would he be willing to part from his new friend for four days? They had not skipped many evenings together for at least three weeks.

"And miss an opportunity to share my exquisite culinary skills?" His toothy grin exhibited self-confidence and humor.

Hearing the foreign sound of my Dad's laughter chime in, he added, "And by sharing, Syd means showing off." Followed by another chuckle. My Dad, too, had Syd pegged for what he was. A braggart, capable of entertaining, cooking, and still remaining lovable. You had to love Sydney Cabel.

"I object. The Shepards are well aware of my areas of expertise. And I believe *you* told *me* that they were expecting me to help prepare an unforgettable feast," Syd's victorious smile spread across his face in triumph.

My Dad lifted his hands to surrender, but had to have the last word, "True, but you must prepare traditional Thanksgiving dishes. Are you up for *that* challenge?" This time Dad appeared the victor. Everyone knew Syd's prowess was in foreign cuisine, not turkey and mashed potatoes. This would make for an interesting meal.

Exactly one week later I found myself packed and ready to board a flight to the Equality State. Dad and Syd were thumbing through magazines from the airport gift shop while I tried loading a movie onto my Netflix account before we boarded. I had chosen *Girls Just Want to Have Fun* starring Sarah Jessica Parker. Alexandra and I had watched it countless times in our elementary years. Perfect for setting my mood to spend a long weekend with my Wyoming friends.

We boarded quickly and without query from flight attendants. They must have been saving themselves for some more likely victims behind us. I got comfy in my window seat and clicked play on my movie. I remember the first quarter of the movie. Then I slipped into a drowsy stupor and fell asleep, dreaming of old friends and docile puppies.

Alexandra and I did not stop talking from the moment we embraced in a familiar hug at the door, to the texts we were sharing as I drove out of her neighborhood a few days later. Catching up on Wyoming gossip took the first half of our stay. Filling her in on my new existence was abbreviated to include only relevant information. I did not realize until I said his name out loud how significant Josh had become in my life. Even his puppies had become an essential part of my new life. Alexandra probably listened to me prattle on and on about Josh and the golden doodles for an eternity before falling asleep in the middle of her bedroom floor. Then we woke in the morning and I continued our babble. She of course was extremely interested in Syd and his current acquaintance. I loved Syd for always contributing to my social status without even meaning to. My friends loved him.

Alexandra and I talked minimally about my mother. She knew me well enough to know her support came in listening, and not asking questions. Besides, what could she say to make me feel better? Her home was open for my family. Her mom was like a mom to me. What else did I need over the long holiday weekend?

Syd proved himself as a culinary genius as we all sat down to feast on traditional Thanksgiving dishes with his added flare. My favorites were the roasted rosemary carrots and pumpkin ravioli, but everyone raved about the roasted duck. Of course, Syd would refuse to serve turkey. I loved that the Shepards handed their kitchen over to Syd, as if he were a celebrity chef visiting.

And then it was over. My trip to Wyoming to celebrate Thanksgiving ended before I had even settled into a comfortable penchant. We landed back at Lambert International Airport late Sunday night. School in less than twelve hours weighing on my jet lagged brain. Luckily, my resplendent spirit would carry me through the next couple of weeks. I craved returning already but was content with the weightless feeling my heart currently carried.

My alarm jolted me from a dream I had not conjured for a couple of weeks. The aesthetic lake reflected the darkening sky above without a single ripple. I sat alone wearing my pajamas and the locket I thought was broken. Funny how dreams seem to only last two or three seconds.

Dismissing the image, I readied myself for what was going to most definitely be a long Monday.

The humdrum feeling settled itself so heavily I considered acting sick to have an additional day off. I reluctantly shook the idea and descended the stairs to find a little breakfast in the kitchen. I was greeted by Marcus. Just Marcus. Slightly awkward. His smile was sheepish, but friendly.

He pulled a chair from the table for me, "Good morning. Sorry I did not know you were still here. I would have made you some toast. Or coffee. Or pancakes. Or...what do girls like to eat when they're late for school?" His words struck me as amusing. Is this how I sounded as I rambled on? His nonsense gave me confidence.

I replied with a genuine smile, "I have time for breakfast." I chose a ripened banana from the counter and seated myself in the chair he had offered. "Bananas and cereal are my breakfast of choice. However, I do enjoy piles of pancakes when Syd has time for making breakfast." I looked down at my hands as I methodically peeled the banana. "I guess you knew Syd made amazing pancakes though." My statement came out as a question. My sudden curiosity revealed itself as I found

an interest in how well Marcus knew my Uncle Syd. I
snuck a peek at him as he took his time forming an
answer. Probably thinking about how to suitably answer
a teenager. I giggled internally. My phone vibrated and
dinged a text. Marcus was saved.

*Hey! Welcome back to MO. Do you want to come over
for dinner tonight?*

A morning message from Josh, plus an interesting
conversation with my uncle's boyfriend. This sullen
Monday took a three sixty, and I had only been out of bed
twenty minutes.

My reply required some level of casualness.
Unlike the excitement I was feeling by his invitation. I
chewed my banana and considered how to word my
response. Syd's arrival interrupted my thoughts. He
appeared in the doorway looking like a cover model for
GQ. My sideways glance at Marcus proved he agreed.
Syd wore business casual like most men wore tuxedos.
He looked dashing with slightly damp hair and well
moisturized skin. How very feminine. More internal
giggling.

Syd grinned at me, but addressed Marcus, "Good
morning, Sunshine!"

Marcus regained his confidence when he spoke to
Syd, "Anna and I would like some pancakes for breakfast.
She tells me you make the best." He winked at me and
whispered for Syd to hear, "He will say he is late to work,
but he'll make it up to us later. Probably offer to make us
filet mignon tonight." Turning to see Syd's reaction, he

rewarded us with a huge, award-winning smile.

"You are right about my pancake skills, the fact I am late, and I will absolutely make it up to you both tonight. Filet mignon is it?" Looking at me now for approval, I remembered Josh was waiting for my text.

Tossing my banana peel into the trashcan, I stood and hugged them both. "Sorry lovebirds, I have a date tonight too. Josh invited me to their house." I picked up my backpack, slipped my coat on, grabbed my keys, and trotted out the door. Over my shoulder I added for good measure, "Make sure Dad is invited to your dinner party."

Josh would surely enjoy this message.

Can I please have dinner at your house? Syd and marcus have a bit too much mirth for a monday. My family is demented. Lol

Even though I was also feeling merry, I hoped to sound a tiny bit needy. As if I needed to be rescued.

He texted back instantly.

Demented is the new black. See you in class ☺

Fifteen expeditious hours later I ticked off all the interesting events that formed my Monday. From the amusing breakfast with Syd and his company, to a lax school day with minimal note taking or homework assignments, followed by dinner and puppy time with Josh and his family. Topping it was coming home to a cheerful Dad chatting about his success at being awarded a huge job the company had bid. We sat on the couch with the television muted for close to an hour. The last time we sat there was the night of the intruder when Officer Adair asked so many questions. I chose not to mention that. I was enjoying Dad's lightheartedness and wanted to prolong our conversation with positive reverie. Finally, he kissed the crown of my head and retired.

I stretched out in my bed replaying my evening with Josh and those adorable puppies. Drowsiness set in as I absorbed the darkness and silence. Then my phone chimed the familiar sound of angel wings and my heart vaulted so forcefully it hurt. I was instantly wide awake and grabbing for my phone.

I am happy for you, Anna.

My heart continued racing, but I managed to type back.

I have a lot to tell you, Mom!

I rolled to my side so I could comfortably text and remain horizontal. The replies always came the second I released my finger from the send button.

I know, love. Give me some details.

Of course, she knew. Which made my heart rate increase even more.

How do you know? I mean how does that work?

This reply came quick too, but after a whole two

seconds passed. She must have had to put thought into the answer.

Your heart cries out to me. You'll understand. But for now, details please.

We texted until I must have finally fallen asleep. I remember describing how Alexandra convinced me to apply for Kansas University so the two of us could be roommates. I told her how Dad had a company install a security system while we were in Wyoming. My favorite was explaining how Josh blushed twelve shades of red when he officially asked if he could be my boyfriend. I think I managed to remain my normal paleness when I smiled and agreed.

Dad startled me awake Tuesday morning by placing a cold hand on my shoulder.

"Anna, did you oversleep? It is almost eight o'clock." He gently squeezed my arm and smiled. Processing his smile and my lateness was like seeing the sunshine during a downpour. He was normally overly concerned with punctuality.

I felt around my mattress for my phone that served as my alarm clock. Finding it under my pillow rather than plugged into its charger explained its neglect on waking me at six thirty. I wondered how late I stayed up texting Mom. I felt an immediate surge of guilt for my ability to communicate with her and my Dad left to his silent grieving. Or maybe she was texting him too and he was keeping that information to himself like I was.

I looked up to my **Dad's** blank eyes. Shadows hid his grief. I was fairly certain Mom was not messaging him. He would wake with purpose like I had found myself doing recently. Her words kept me strong while Dad still barely managed to stay afloat.

"Sorry, Dad, my alarm didn't go off. I can be ready and out the door in ten minutes." I was already in my closet looking for a clean uniform skirt. I could pull my hair into a ponytail and eat while I drove. I would only be fifteen minutes late.

Dad's calm reply slowed my hasty movements. "It snowed early this morning, but only about an inch. I doubt they'll be counting anyone tardy. Take your time driving." He exited my room to give me privacy to change, but hollered back, "Do you want me to drop you off, so you don't have to worry about the road conditions? I could easily drop you off on my way to the plant." His offer came as he moved down the stairs causing me to continue my hurried attempts of making myself presentable.

I dressed, brushed both my teeth and hair, and made my way to the kitchen before he even finished pouring his coffee. His coat was on, so I knew he was ready to head out. I took two granola bars from the pantry and answered his question while pouring a small glass of milk. "I do want you to drop me off at school." He smiled broadly and I felt this simple gesture of accepting his ride invitation would brighten his day. I needed to find more ways to help build him back to the man he was such a short time ago. I quickly drained the milk and put my coat on. In less than nine minutes after waking, I was following Dad to the garage ready for my Tuesday. "I bet I can get a ride home at three o'clock, so no need to pick me up after school."

He nodded and started his truck. "That would be great. I have a meeting that is scheduled for four o'clock, so I might not be home until six or so." We pulled out of the garage and I was immediately awestruck by the beauty of our neighborhood blanketed in a thin layer of soft white snow. Yesterday's heavy cloud cover had dropped its load and cleared. Bright sunshine touched the ground causing the yards and rooftops to sparkle. It was beautiful. Snow was nothing new to my senses. My childhood in Wyoming had seen plenty of days off school due to snow. We would sled, build snowmen, and have snowball fights. However, now I focused on the beauty of the blue skies contrasting with the white landscape. I knew no schools were released due to road conditions and was secretly happy that little kids wouldn't be out destroying the perfectly smooth surfaces of the snow. Dad drove cautiously despite the clean pavement.

I approached the main entrance alongside two other students that were dropped off by parents. I followed them to the office, not sure the protocol for tardiness. I was pleasantly surprised to find the hallway adorned with dozens of poinsettias and a familiar song playing overhead on the PA system. It was a song I had heard at Mass when we attended over the long weekend. Advent had begun, marking a new season in the church's liturgical calendar. In less time than it took to inhale I realized how close we were to Christmas and that it would be the first without my Mom. The last poinsettia I had seen was at our home in Wyoming. The last Christmas gift I opened was selected by my Mom. Breathe, Anna. You can handle this, I told myself. The silent encouragement got me to the office, checked in, and with tardy slip in hand, seated in first hour. Exhale.

Five hours and five classes later I was reminded that the letter to a loved one was due tomorrow. Despite my interest in literature and journalism, writing this letter seemed arbitrary. Was the teacher planning on grading it and expecting us to then deliver it to the individual? Mailing a personal note to Alexandra's Mom seemed fitting, given she had just hosted our family for Thanksgiving. However, it also seemed a little too personal for a teacher to read and edit beforehand. Suddenly, thinking back to my morning with Dad, I shifted gears instantaneously. I needed to write my letter to him. He would benefit from my heartfelt words and hopefully be a fraction less despondent after reading them. Who cares what the teacher thought? This assignment was timed perfectly, and I knew just who to ask for help with my words.

7 DECEMBER

I made myself comfortable under the covers after showering and brushing my teeth. I tucked a notebook and pen under my pillows and settled into my bed. I browsed a couple of my favorite online shopping sites trying to keep myself alert. I couldn't let myself fall asleep anytime soon. She just had to text me tonight. A standard tri-tone alert startled me. A message from Josh appeared, so I tapped it abandoning my shopping.

Do you want to help me pick out a christmas tree tomorrow? We always get a live one from our land.

I was thankful this arrived as a text and we were not having an actual conversation. I had purposefully put decorating for Christmas out of my mind. Digging through boxes of ornaments, stockings, Nativity sets, and holiday photos was at the bottom of the list of things I wanted to do. And I was certain Dad would ignore the approaching holiday altogether.

Not sure my family will be in the spirit of the holiday this year. Thnx for asking. Maybe I could tag along when you chop yours down?

Surely Josh would understand the lack of

motivation Dad, Syd, and I would be demonstrating towards decorating. I bet he put some thought into sending me this invitation, so I added…

I could help you decorate your tree?

His reply took longer to appear. He probably felt bad for thinking that decorating our house was a good idea.

I would absolutely love for you to help us decorate! I know this season will be hard. Let me know what I can do to make it easier. <3

His sweet words made me smile. Helping his family would be less painful than touching our holiday memories. I was composing my reply mentally when the familiar sound of shattered glass mixed with angel wings filled my ears and delicately vibrated my palm. I knew she would text.

How was your day, anna?

I abandoned my conversation with Josh and wasted no time with a greeting. I wanted Mom help with my assignment, and was eager for her wise words to help.

Mom, i have to write a letter to dad for a class. I want to say something that will help him heal. Losing u has broken him. I want him to live knowing you still love us and that it is ok for him to be happy. Can you help me?

As always, the reply came in a blink.

Anna, you amaze me. You underestimate your own

strength and wisdom. This assignment is an expression of your love. Keep your message simple. You are right about the fact I still love you both. Love endures all things, even death. And when you are with me again you will see the power of love.

Her words helped but left me curious. Will love feel different when we die? I replied back after thinking...

Thank you. So, keep the letter simple. Say I love you. Remind him we're still a family, just separated by time instead of space. Does love feel different where you are?

I am positive my question sounded juvenile, even trivial. Surely an emotion remained simply an emotion. However, she said I would *see* the power of her love when we reunited.

Interminable. Immeasurable. Indescribable.

Her reply came fast, and just three words. I refrained from asking any further questions. I sat up in my bed and created a lap desk with a pillow. While her words hung in mind, I wanted to start the letter to Dad. Holding the pen with too much tension in my grip, I intentionally inhaled and mindfully relaxed before the first word appeared on the blue line. The letter seemed to write itself from that point on. Keeping simple in mind, and Mom's advice close at heart, I finished in minutes and made no changes after proofreading my work three times.

Dear Dad,

The struggles we have faced in the last few months are greatly overshadowed by my love for you. The distance between the two of us, and the wife and Mom we miss, is measured in memories, not miles. Imagining her smile and listening for the sound of her laughter in my mind is comforting. Just like oxygen is necessary for our earthly existence, her continued love is necessary, and will never cease to exist. Her indispensable love is my oxygen. God has a plan for us that includes being with Mom again. While we endure the void of her presence, you and I can also find happiness in the anticipation of that reunion. I love you, Dad, and I know Mom does too. Love endures all things, even death. Let's live in her love.

Love, Anna

Staring at the notebook brought tears to my eyes. The unfairness of what our life had become suddenly felt overwhelming. Why did I even have to say things like this to my Dad? My classmates were probably all writing letters to their boyfriends or girlfriends. While they decorated their assignment with doodles of hearts and smiley faces, I covered my page with fresh tears. I missed Mom so much, and here I sat, trying to console my widowed father. Life sucked. Death sucked.

Anna, your words are perfect. Go to sleep. You are tired.

As I read my angel's final message for the night, a speck of light filtered through my tears. Without her help I would be worthless. I squeezed my phone in my palm and wrapped my arms around myself. I cried myself into a peaceful sleep. My dream by the lake reinvented itself. The water sparkled a deep blue-green. I sat barefoot alongside both of my parents who were laughing at the unusual colors of the animals surrounding the water. Pink birds, blue turtles, and a very familiar green puppy.

Bundled in my favorite winter gear I had picked out two years ago in Wyoming, I walked behind Josh across frozen earth hunting for a perfect Christmas tree. As I followed him, I could faintly hear him humming the tune of O Christmas Tree. My thoughts immediately wandered back to our family traditions that would no longer exist even though I promised myself I wouldn't go there. The sights, sounds, and smells of this season were going to be torture.

"How about this one?" Josh's question interrupted my thoughts. I studied his tree choice by circling it twice looking it up and down and scrutinizing playfully.

"This tree would be perfect if it were a foot taller, had straighter branches, and sagged a little less around the bottom." I smiled as he stared at the tree, absorbing my critique.

After a few seconds he looked at me accusingly and replied, "If we wanted a tree to fit all those requirements, we would have to shop for one in a department store." I saw a satisfied smirk on his face as he turned and moved on, surveying for another candidate. I trailed along, thinking more about spending this time with Josh, and less about the tree. Obviously, I was not focused enough on my walking. Despite having on a pair of quality hiking boots, I tripped over an exposed tree root and caught myself with both hands as I fell clumsily to the cold ground. Josh turned instantly at the sound of my body hitting the forest floor.

"Anna!" he cried. His warm body was at my side before I had a chance to push up off my dirty and scathed palms. "Let me help you."

I raised to a seated position and examined my hands. No blood, thankfully, but dozens of tiny white lines appeared where the roots had torn a layer of my skin. Feeling embarrassment instead of pain, I glanced up to Josh and said pathetically, "I haven't always been the most graceful person." A lump formed in my throat, but I swallowed hard and held back my tears.

Josh sat down facing me and took both of my shaking hands in his. He peered at the injury, and then lifted my hands to his lips one at a time and gently kissed each palm. The lump in my throat sank to my stomach and immediately became a feeling of butterflies. Josh looked straight in my eyes. His calm words erased my embarrassment and left me wishing I might stumble again and again. "I'm sorry I wasn't here to catch you." I blushed deeply and looked down again at my broken skin. My palms felt sweaty where his kisses were tattooed. I reversed my hands so that I was able to squeeze his softly.

At eight o'clock my Dad texted, wondering if I was planning to come home. Remembering that Syd had plans with Marcus and knowing Dad didn't like being home alone, guilt washed over me immediately.

Be home in 30 min. xoxo

I looked from my phone's screen to Josh, and then to the tree we had magnificently decorated. It was beautifully lit with white lights and adorned with a mixture of metallic snowflakes and tiny framed family photos. As I helped attach each of the pictures, I saw Josh grow from an infant to school aged boy. Every picture was taken with him and Santa at the local mall. Each frame allowed me a peek at his past, obviously filled with love and attention from his adoring parents. As we decorated the tree, Mrs. Justice recounted adorable things Josh had said to Santa while sitting on his lap. My favorite was when she said Josh asked Santa for a new kindergarten teacher because his was mean.

"Everything okay?" Josh asked, sitting down beside me, peeking at my phone. "You are quiet all of a sudden." His gaze moved back to my eyes and stayed there until I finally answered.

"My Dad is home alone. I need to go." I took another look at their Christmas tree, and added, "This was fun. I'm glad you invited me to be part of your family this afternoon and evening." I stood slowly, hoping he would tug me back for a few more minutes, but instead he stood too. We walked to the front hall where Josh lifted my coat from the hook and offered to assist my arms in finding their sleeves. I zipped the front and found my driving gloves in the pockets but hesitated to put them on. I wasn't ready to say goodbye.

"I appreciate you being here to help. I apologize if my Mom bored you by recapping my childhood." His eyes met mine, and for a few seconds I could not breathe. "Maybe next time you're here she will get out the home movies," he added, almost as a promise. Knowing the invitation to return was already extended, I exhaled and knew it was time to get home to my Dad.

I carefully pulled my gloves over my sore palms. Noticing my reluctance to pull my gloves on normally, Josh again raised my hands and kissed each one.

"Text me when you're home, I need to know you are safe." Letting go of my hands, he turned to the door and opened it for me. I walked by without a word. My farewell would come later when I was curled up, cozy in bed. That would give me a chance to decide how to respond to his affectionate goodbye.

December rounded its corner more quickly than I could have asked for. My family's lack of holiday festivities actually catapulted us through the month without letting us dwell on our grief. Syd insisted we at least put up a Christmas tree. So, Dad and I sat on the couch eating Doritos while Syd and Marcus dragged a box containing a six-foot artificial tree into the living room. While we munched away, the two of them assembled the tree, strung the lights, and hung ornaments. It was the only sign our house bore indicating it was in fact Christmastime. My Mother would not have approved of this tree. But it was entertaining, nonetheless, witnessing my Uncle's glee while decorating. I am pretty sure he missed his call as some kind of interior decorator. Too bad he was in the concrete business, I doubt he exhibited this excitement mixing sand, gravel, cement, and water.

"You two could help, we have over a hundred gold stars to put on this masterpiece," Syd spoke with his back turned to Dad and me. We turned to each other, smiled, and both took another handful of chips. Our reply came in the form of crunching that Syd registered as a "no thanks." His feelings were definitely not hurt. He made himself busy inspecting the work Marcus had completed without giving us a second thought. I had to admit, their tree was coming along beautifully. It glistened from top to bottom with white lights and gold ornaments. There was absolutely nothing about this tree that even remotely reminded me of a traditional Cabel family Christmas tree. My Mother painstakingly found a branch for every ornament we had collected over the two decades my parents had been married. By the time she was finished, the tree itself was invisible, hidden behind hundreds of mismatched ornaments. It too was magnificent, but not in the way Syd's tree shone. I admired his determination in creating some holiday cheer. And I silently applauded his effort of keeping our traditions boxed up, safe in the attic.

I woke up around nine on Christmas morning. Attending midnight Mass, the night before had wiped me out. The Mass was beautiful; long, but beautiful. A choir sang every Christmas song I could think of, plus at least ten more. We returned home after one in the morning, and I went straight to bed. I had seen Josh at Mass, and briefly talked to him while my Dad spoke with his parents. He promised to text later, but I turned my phone off, wanting nothing but sleep, and an end to this month. Then changing my mind, I powered my phone on again, and sent a quick message so he did not think me too rude.

Merry Christmas, Josh. Hope I see you again over break. Xo

I turned my phone off without waiting for his reply. Surely, he would assume I was asleep if I did not answer any text he might send back.

I found a comfortable spot on my pillow, and allowed myself to breathe deeply, enjoying the silence of my room. The Christmas choir was echoing in my memory, but that too was peaceful. And as if on cue, my phone vibrated and chimed with angel wings.

Merry Christmas, Anna. You are in my heart.

Without a doubt, this was the most amazing gift a girl could receive. A message straight from heaven. With trembling fingers, I typed back.

It is not the same without you here. I love and miss you. Merry Christmas. Xoxo

I waited for a message to return, but no message came. I fell asleep with my phone in hand, smiling like a little kid waiting for Santa.

Taking my time to wake up properly, I stayed in bed until almost ten o'clock. I finally heard movement downstairs. Wrapping myself in a fleece blanket, I wandered down the stairs anticipating nothing out of the ordinary on this Christmas morning. Surprisingly, I found my Dad dressed, sipping coffee, and looking quite cheerful. He smiled as I entered the kitchen.

"Merry Christmas, Anna!" his greeting was genuine and accompanied with a huge smile and outstretched arms. Pushing back his chair, he stood, and I walked right into his hug.

Our embrace lasted a full minute before I finally looked up at him and said, "Merry Christmas to you too." I moved toward the kitchen table, pulling my blanket along with me. I sat in the chair securely wrapped, hoping my Dad would offer me cereal, seeing that I was trapped in my blanket. Instead he informed me that Syd was planning to make a feast when he woke up. "Will he make me some French toast?" This Christmas morning wasn't going to be so bad after all.

"I would imagine Syd could be talked into anything, especially a request as simple as French toast," Dad answered as he took another sip of coffee. "I can pour you some coffee or juice while you wait for food," he offered. Standing again he found a mug and poured coffee before giving me a chance to respond to his question. Habit, I would assume. He and Mom always enjoyed their morning rituals. I accepted the mug by freeing my hands from their blanket prison.

"What are we going to do today?" I asked, as if it were a typical question, asked on a typical Saturday morning.

Dad took a deep breath and answered only after putting thought into his response. "Well, after Syd feeds us, and offers us seconds and thirds, we should maybe do something out of the ordinary." He looked down at his hands while he spoke. "I was thinking about visiting the cemetery. I would love for you to go with me, but understand if you…" His words trailed off into silence. He kept his gaze directed at his hands that were wrapped around his mug.

"Of course, I will go," I reassured. Moving my hands away from the warmth of my own coffee, I gently squeezed his. He exhaled audibly and broke from his trance. "We could take a poinsettia," I offered.

"That sounds perfect," he smiled slightly, not even taking time to mull over the idea. "Flowers would be the most adequate gift I could offer Elenora. Thank you, Anna."

Then quite abruptly, my Dad stood and retreated from the kitchen table to his bedroom. As he walked away, he called back, "Don't move, I have something for you." I sat perplexed for less than a minute before he returned, carrying a small, beautifully wrapped gift box. "Open it" were his words. In the few seconds he had disappeared and returned, my Dad appeared to have regained his cheerfulness. It did not seem fabricated, but quite sincere. I accepted the package he placed in front of me, studying it quizzically. My thoughts were curious not only for what it contained, but also when he had found time to shop.

"Open it," he repeated, this time with a softer

tone in his voice. Dad sat back down and remained motionless, staring at me, his cheerful grin intact.

Without haggling, I carefully picked up the package observing its weightlessness. Using my fingernail to separate the tape from the box, I was meticulous not to damage the perfect bow. I set the wrapping to the side and next was able to admire the box itself that still hid my gift. The black box was embossed with an ornate design of leaves that vined around the word Paragon. I immediately treasured this box, not even knowing what it contained. My understanding of a paragon was something of perfection, or excellence. The seconds it took to open the box seemed like minutes as my curiosity peaked. I removed the lid and was awestruck with what was revealed. A silver locket rested on the tiniest of silk pillows secured in place by thin gold string. Unlike my broken locket hidden away upstairs in my drawer, this one was rectangular rather than heart shaped. My initials were delicately monogrammed on the front in looped cursive lettering. Gingerly untying the gold thread, my hands shook unnoticeably as I removed the necklace from its treasure box. It was indeed perfect, truly paragon.

Dad continued to stare as I unclasped the locket and opened it. Two empty frames nudged at the emptiness in my heart this morning.

Intuitively, Dad spoke in a whisper, "You have so many people that love you. I could not decide whose picture deserved a place in this necklace. I hope you don't think I'm so lazy that I didn't properly complete your gift. I wanted you to decide who belongs in each frame that will be worn so close to your heart." I know he was attempting not to tear up as he said this. I reciprocated with similar sentiment, not wanting our Christmas morning to be too heavy with grief. He had chosen an amazing gift and was entitled to my contented gratitude.

Our family of three drove through the cemetery under a bright blue sky. Much like that of the day we buried my Mom, this day too was clear and sunny. With this Christmas Day measuring above average on the thermometer, I was overwhelmed with the memory of her funeral. Not wanting Dad to see my fresh tears, I dug through the drawstring bag on the car seat beside me searching for nothing in particular. Dad and Syd sat in the front seat discussing dinner plans as we departed the cemetery.

"Let's start a new tradition," Syd was saying. "Christmas dinner from the freezer. I can bake a frozen lasagna, I know we have frozen bread dough, and ice cream for dessert." He turned in his car seat looking back at me for approval.

I swallowed hard and willed my tears to cease. "You deserve a night of easy meal prep," I managed to offer. "Lasagna sounds good, but I'm not really hungry yet." I looked skyward again and suddenly craved being outdoors in this brilliant sunshine. "It's so warm outside for a Christmas Day, we should go walk somewhere," I suggested.

Syd's face lit up as he added to my idea. "Marcus and I run in Tower Grove Park. It's only about fifteen minutes from here. How does that sound?"

Dad must have accepted this as our new plan because he picked up his phone and asked it for directions to the park.

"Speaking of Marcus, how about I tell him we're planning a lasagna feast, and he will bring some salad, or fresh bread, or wine, or…" Syd stopped midsentence. Phone in hand, he was presumably texting Marcus, planning our evening.

My own phone vibrated and looking down I was instantly ebullient.

Merry Christmas! I was wondering if i could stop by in a bit? I have something for you. :)

Of course, he would have something for me. I had nothing. "Can I invite Josh tonight?" At the very least I could feed him I thought.

Hearing Dad's reply intensified the prospect of the evening. "The more the merrier, of course he can come," his voice steady, almost eager for an added guest. My guess, Dad's way of avoiding thinking about what a normal Cabel Christmas would have included. He looked up into the rear-view mirror making eye contact with me. His eyes were simultaneously despondent and hopeful. How was that even possible? I tried smiling at his reflection in the mirror then looked down to my phone to text Josh.

Hi! Merry Christmas to you too. We are going to walk at tower grove park. Want to join us?

While I waited for Josh to reply I returned to the front seat conversation. Marcus had replied and said he would be at our house by six with salad, wine, and a cheesecake. Perfect pairing for lasagna according to Syd. Dad continued driving without contributing to any more of the planning. Obviously lost in thought, or maybe retreating from all thought.

Josh's reply pinged my phone.

Enjoy your walk. I will be by your house in a couple hours. Text me when you are home.

I would enjoy our walk. What better way to avoid overthinking this holiday.

Lasagna and cheesecake at 6. Please come hungry.

Josh immediately sent back a thumbs up. I looked up from my screen and said to Syd, "Please make sure Marcus knows Josh will be joining us." Syd simply replied with his stellar grin.

Three miles and three coffees later, we were driving toward our warm home. The temperature had dropped considerably after the sun dropped below the horizon. I held my latte with two hands trying to heat my palms. The sky had transformed from its watery blue to vivid stripes of navy, purple, and deep orange. Admiring the view and thinking about the conversation we'd had while walking, a feeling of contentment settled in my core. I had almost survived my first motherless Christmas. Dad seemed at peace as he walked and was now humming along with the radio station. I touched the empty locket hanging around my neck. I needed to give Dad a gift, but shopping today was out of the question. Without another second passing, the thought of my English assignment popped to mind. The letter I had written Dad all those weeks ago sat unread in my notebook. Hopefully he would find value in those simple words. As soon as we pulled into the garage, I was on a mission to find it. I set my latte on a table in the living room and bolted upstairs two at a time in pursuit of my backpack. Taking less than a minute to locate the letter, I returned to the kitchen before Dad and Syd even made their way into the house.

The letter was neatly removed from the notebook and folded in thirds. I handed it to Dad as he walked through the kitchen toward his bedroom.

"Dad, I wrote this letter for you," I said in a hushed tone. Sensing my urgency to gift my father with something so personal, Syd politely exited the room.

Not knowing how to react, my Dad set his coffee on the kitchen table and accepted the folded paper. "I didn't shop for any gifts for our holiday, and I'm sorry for that. When I passed stores with decorations, or playing Christmas music, I couldn't stomach going in and looking for presents," I paused and let Dad settle his eyes on my letter. "I love you and want you to be happy. I hope my words mean as much to you as this locket does to me." I gently put my hand over the necklace. I thought for a second about his invitation for filling it with my choice of photographs. Would I ever fill those two tiny frames?

Dad kept the letter folded, clutched in his hand. He stepped forward and hugged me tight for most of a minute. Then turned and walked to his room without saying a word. As he retreated to his room, I could tell from his posture he intended to read my gift now.

I moved to the living room to find my latte, my phone, and a blanket. Until Josh arrived, I wanted to enjoy some silence. I spent a few minutes answering texts I had received earlier that day from Wyoming friends, and some sent from my new classmates that had quickly become friends. Each message sounded similar in sentiment; wishing my family a Merry Christmas and many prayers and hugs coming my way. I replied to each friend with the same generic message and a cheerful little Santa Claus emoji so they wouldn't all picture me completely depressed and teary. When that task was finished, I opened YouTube, knowing there would be multiple new videos to keep my attention.

I was startled when the doorbell rang. Before I had time to dig myself free from my blanket, Syd made his way from the kitchen to the front door. Opening it wide for Marcus who entered carrying armloads of groceries, we were both greeted with an enormous smile.

"Merry Christmas, Cabels!" his voiced echoed loud enough for passersby on the street to hear clearly. His jovial mood was infectious. Syd grabbed one bag of groceries and hugged Marcus with his other arm. I made my way over and joined the embrace just as Dad walked in, also smiling.

"What are all these groceries?" Syd demanded, "You were assigned cheesecake, salad, and wine!" He took both bags from Marcus and without waiting for a reply, strolled to the kitchen. He turned back expecting to see Marcus follow in his wake. Marcus hesitated, however, still looking in my direction.

Before following Syd to the kitchen, Marcus spoke to me. "When I was walking up the front steps, a red truck pulled into your driveway. You should go greet *your* guest," Marcus relayed this bit of information in a sing-song voice that made me feel like I had a crush on a boy in junior high school. Or, that he knew something I did not.

I turned to face the window in the front door only to be startled again by a figure there, staring back at me. My surprise replaced immediately with joy when I focused on the smile Josh was wearing. I opened the glass door, but Josh didn't make an attempt to come inside.

"Do you have a coat handy? It's gotten cold out here," Josh said without losing his smile.

Goosebumps raised on my arms just from the ten seconds the door had been open. The air was still, and with no wind, the neighborhood was silent. "Why are you standing there? Come in out of the cold, and Merry Christmas!" I felt myself blushing despite the chill. The affect Josh had on me was often overwhelming. I felt myself holding my breath while I waited for his reply, or more importantly, his entrance.

Without even realizing my Dad had approached, he startled me for the third time in five minutes by wrapping a coat over my shoulders. It seemed Marcus wasn't the only one who knew something I did not. Now Dad was coercing me outside into the cold. And an unfamiliar, almost gleeful smile, was spread across his face as he escorted us both outside.

"I'm confused," was all I could stutter. My socked feet padded softly on the dry concrete sidewalk as I was being guided toward Josh's truck. I slipped my arms into the sleeves of the coat that draped over me. "I don't think it's very polite to yank a girl away from her warm latte and cozy blanket to walk out to the truck on this cold blustery evening. Surely Marcus or Syd can help you carry in whatever it is you need help with…" Both Josh and my Dad continued smiling and marching forward.

"Don't be silly, Anna, the leaves left in the trees aren't even rustling. Compared to a Wyoming Christmas, it feels almost tropical out here," Dad chided.

Josh let go of my hand he had been tugging on to get me outside. He opened the passenger side door of his truck. When the interior dash light illuminated the cab, I could see a sturdy wooden crate that filled the space I had sat in a few times when Josh had invited me to ride along with him to his house. Remembering now he said he had something for me, my curiosity swelled. Josh gripped the crate securely and slid it out of the cab and placed it on the driveway at my feet. There was no lid, so I could instantly see what lay inside. My favorite golden doodle. She was curled in a ball sound asleep; a red bow fastened to her collar.

I stared at the sleeping pup for a few seconds, or maybe several minutes, it was hard to think right then. Her fur was neatly groomed, all brushed in the same direction allowing the natural waves to show. Her breathing was almost unnoticeable.

"Anna?" Josh whispered. "She's yours to keep if you want to adopt her." I didn't look at Josh as he spoke, I couldn't take my eyes off this perfect little ball of fur. Tears slowly formed, limiting my vision until I blinked, and they fell down both cheeks. More tears followed accompanied by a rasping breath, and then a silent sob. I finally reached down and carefully cradled the puppy in my two hands. Scooping upward, heedful not to abruptly awaken her, I pulled her to my chest like a mother protecting an infant. I continued to stare and remain silent. Holding her close I suddenly became aware of my own heartbeat. I hope she could not feel its vibration as it pounded in my chest.

"I think she's in shock, Josh," I heard my Dad say with amusement evident in his voice.

Josh's reply, however, was of concern, "Is that good or bad?"

Dad didn't answer, so I was forced to speak, reassuring Josh that this was in fact *good.* "Happy tears," I managed to squeak out. Josh visibly exhaled and smiled with relief.

I was up at two in the morning still texting Alexandra my details of the holiday. She had been filled in on my empty locket, Josh's visit, and my nameless puppy. Keeping up with Wyoming news was always fascinating too. Despite being states away, my friends seemed close when I was so thoroughly informed.

Checking the time, and realizing it was a few short hours until sunup, I wished Alexandra a final good night message. I plugged my cell phone into its charger and laid my head on my pillow. I had anticipated a message from my Mom the entire evening into these early morning hours but was left disappointed. A message had been sent late on Christmas Eve which now seemed days ago. My holiday had been eventful, and I wanted to chat. I assumed however, that she knew about my day. I left my ringer turned on with full volume just in case a message appeared. Falling asleep soon after, I had no dreams, rather, restless tossing carried me into the later morning hours.

I bounded out of bed around eight when the thought of my puppy came to mind. I had not heard any barking yet and hoped I would find her curled up in her kennel still snoozing. Tiptoeing through the house in an attempt to not wake Dad or Syd, I made my way to the laundry room where we had created a doggy habitat. Complete with cushion, toys, food bowls, and a hook for her leash, the laundry room now looked more like a pet supply store than anything else. My Dad had been part of the scheming with Josh to make us dog owners. He agreed to accept Josh's gift with excitement. Listening to the two of them describe the multiple conversations that had taken place, and how many near blunders almost ruined the surprise made us laugh aloud the night before. Evidently, I had walked in the kitchen a few days ago while Dad was on the phone discussing kennel sizes.

I found my little friend sprawled on her cushion, and still sound asleep. I sat admiring her without opening her kennel so that she would continue resting. Josh had said puppies were like newborns and slept more than they were wakeful. I used this time to consider name options. This too, was a big part of last night's conversation. Both Dad and Syd had suggested adorable little girl names, while Josh and Marcus suggested names that seemed overused for the dog population. My desire for name selection was to choose a unique, yet meaningful title suitable for an adorable canine that would be fitting for a tiny pup, and a full-grown golden doodle.

I whispered the name Cheyenne to hear what it sounded like out loud. The little furball twitched slightly. Staring at her delicate curls, I said it a second time to test if she would respond intuitively. She remained still, but I summoned the courage to carefully open her kennel and gently pet her. The latch clicked loudly in the silent house, resulting in the pup's head lifting and turning simultaneously. With alert eyes, she peered at me and lifted her ears slightly. I said Cheyenne a third time, and was rewarded with a barely audible dog sigh, followed by a yawn. My petting hand continued massaging her shoulders and then traveled around to her chin. I used two hands to cradle her body and remove her from her bed.

"Good morning, Cheyenne," I said in a cheerful voice, confirming I had found her name. It was beautiful, perfect for a dog, and full of amazing memories of an amazing place that would be on my mind almost hourly when I called to my new pet.

I nestled Cheyenne in my lap and snapped a quick picture of her with my phone. I sent it to Josh with a message attached.

Cheyenne says hello. Can you visit today and teach me how to take care of my pup?

Figuring Josh was still sleeping and wouldn't reply for a bit, I returned my phone to the pocket of my sweatshirt, and continued gazing at Cheyenne. My fingertips lightly stroked her fur, and her heavy eyelids closed again. I remained motionless to allow her to fall back to sleep. However, we both jumped when my phone vibrated and chimed from where it was trapped in my pocket. Not just a text alert, but *the* text alert I had been impatiently waiting for last night. I did my best to extract my phone while keeping Cheyenne comfortable on my lap.

Such a delightful gift!

Mom did know about my holiday. Her words sent a warm and very pleasant sensation through my body. The idea that this conversation was actually going

to transpire grazed my thoughts momentarily.
Everything I longed to tell her left my mind, and I was
arrested to the notion she already knew, but I still needed
to tell her. I stared blankly at my phone not knowing
what to type.

Did you name her?

Her second attempt to converse challenged my
thoughts. Maybe she was not aware of every detail. My
fingers spelled *Cheyenne*, and I hit send. Before I
blinked her reply appeared.

Perfect. Absolutely perfect.

I wanted to confess to her how eager I was for
Josh to come back and train me to train Cheyenne, but I
hesitated. Instead I chose my words carefully.

*Yesterday did not feel like Christmas. It was memorable,
but it was hard to enjoy because...*

I hadn't even hit send and Mom's words filled my
screen.

*Anna, no one expects you to grieve in a certain way.
Especially me. You have done an outstanding job of
staying strong for your father.*

Putting consideration into her words, I began a
new message.

I miss you.

Expecting an immediate response, I stared at my

lit screen. Nothing. Seconds passed. I noticed my back ached from sitting slouched on the tile floor. I sat up straight, pressing my spine parallel to the wall. A full minute went by and no response. I resigned to the certainty that our conversation had ended when my phone chimed.

Anna, emotions do not exist beyond the life you know. As I said before, my love is timeless. Find comfort in that truth. If lives were free of hurt, there would be no desire to attain an eternal life. It is okay to grieve. Continue being strong.

Tears welled in my eyes but did not drop. I intentionally inhaled and exhaled causing Cheyenne to wake. I set my phone down on the tile floor and carefully picked up my puppy. Raising her gently my eyes lifted, and I was startled to see my Dad sitting at the kitchen table staring at me. How long had he been there?

"Who would make you tearful so early in the morning?" he asked, deep concern coating his voice. He stood then and slowly walked closer to me. "Anna, is everything all right?"

Tears were still dampening the corners of my eyes. The truth to my tears could not be spoken of, but I could not lie to my father.

"Yesterday was *the* best, and *the* worst holiday. I think my emotions are just adjusting to the highs and lows," I said. Hoping my answer would be sufficient I stood with Cheyenne in my arms and walked into the kitchen, passing my Dad, and opening the pantry door.

Trying to change the subject, I added, "Do you think I should go ahead and feed Cheyenne?" Dropping her name would surely distract him.

Dad followed me back to the kitchen and attempted to take the puppy from my possession. Freeing my hands to allow me to prepare her bowls, I handed her over.

"Cheyenne?" he said softly, more to kindle a response from her than to question why I had chosen the name. I remained silent while he processed my name selection. His conclusion made my heart stop, "Perfect. Absolutely perfect."

8 FRIEND

The winter weeks passed slowly, marked by Cheyenne's growth, rather than watching the calendar. By late February she weighed fourteen pounds, slept all night in her kennel, and mastered the commands sit, stay, lay down, and high five. I bragged often of my dog training skills to Dad and Syd, however it was Josh who should take credit. He had established a routine of visiting every day after school to help. Over the last eight weeks we typically spent a couple of hours together each day. After attending to Cheyenne, we studied, helped Syd make dinner, watched Netflix, or occasionally met some friends. I had become so comfortable hanging out with Josh, that I ceased telling my Dad he would be at our house. Josh became a fixture, and likewise, made himself at home, helping himself to snacks, taking charge of the remote, even napping while I folded laundry. It was easy, and familiar, and fun.

A goodnight message from Mom appeared most nights, contributing to my ease and good mood. Even though this was not typical, not even sure if it was even my reality, I grew accustomed to the familiarity of my daily routine.

By March my schedule became so predictable, I

neglected to realize it was so close to my own birthday. Turning eighteen should be a highlight of a senior year. However, the subtle change in my age manifested anxiety. No longer would I be able to say I was weeks or months beyond having a Mother, now it would seem years. I was only seventeen when she died, but now, eighteen, then twenty, then a decade would pass, and I would forget her.

More troubling than turning eighteen was my Dad's new habit. While I had settled into comfort during the evening hours focusing on schoolwork, Cheyenne, and Josh, Dad was increasing the number of glasses of wine he consumed. He and Mom used to enjoy a glass with dinner most nights. Lately, his glass had escalated to two or three, some nights entire bottle. He did not show signs of intoxication, but with my naivety, how would I know? Fearful of turning nothing into something, I refrained from discussing the matter with Syd. He drank bottles of wine anyway and would probably justify my Dad's consumption based on his own. The only other option would be to mention it to Mom if she sent a text soon.

"What does Anna want to do for her birthday?" Syd asked me casually at the breakfast table a few days later. He sat with his hands in his lap, leaning into the table looking at me as I chewed my bagel slowly. His question triggered Dad to turn away from the sink where he was washing his coffee mug and gaze silently in my direction.

I swallowed but remained still. The thought of

my birthday was nauseating. I longed to be a normal teenage girl who had birthday wish lists and high expectations for a day of partying with friends.

"I was anticipating an all-inclusive, seven-day trip to Hawaii," I joked, knowing they would see through this comment. I returned to my bagel hoping the subject would change without me having to be creative so early in the morning.

Dad interjected, however, and made a suggestion that caught me off guard. "Let's go shopping so you can choose something special." He sat down at the table across from me, waiting for a response.

"You hate shopping," I answered. "Remember when you tagged along with Mom and me?" I looked at my food as I continued, "All we heard was complaining. You didn't like our shops, our browsing, walking, you even grumbled when we ordered you a coffee." Thinking back to that experience seemed silly but brought a vacuous smile to my face.

Dad folded his arms across his chest and stared at me with a look of defiance. I could tell by the set of his jaw what he was about to say would be a lie. He was a bad liar. "I love shopping! I always looked forward to the days I spent with my girls squirting perfume, trying on dresses, and sniffing candles." A grin breaking through, betraying his words, "I can't believe you thought I was a complainer. My feelings are hurt." He finished by pouting dramatically.

"Christopher, how dare you mock the talent of our

ladies," Syd inserted. "Shopping is a sport that I have been training them in for years."

Syd turned to me and added, "A shopping date sounds fabulous! Marcus introduced me to a few local shops I know you'll just adore." He took hold of my hand in a plea to say yes to his invitation.

Not wanting to neglect my Dad, or truly hurt his feelings, I decided on the truth. "Honestly, I want to skip my birthday all together and just stay seventeen." I moved my hand away from Syd and folded my napkin into a tiny square, taking my time lining up the edges, trapping the bagel crumbs. Both Dad and Syd sensed the tension in my voice and failed to respond to my comment. Two sets of eyes locked into mine until the silence was unbearable, and I stood to exit the kitchen. Doubling back, I instead retreated to Cheyenne's spot and lifted her gently from the kennel where she was sleeping. I attached her leash and headed out the door without even taking time to put on a jacket.

Cheyenne wiggled free from my arms but remained my captive on her leash. I walked aimlessly away from our house. Stopping briefly every fifteen steps to allow the puppy to sniff around rocks, bushes, and other obstacles in her path. I extracted my phone from my pocket.

Hey want to hang out?

I hit send and stared at my screen hoping for an instant reply from Josh. I strolled another ten minutes before he finally replied.

Can't meet now but call me asap. I might need your help with something!

Interest charged my spirit. Josh seemed to always be involved in fascinating activities. His family was a collection of busy mixed with engaging, always immersed in projects with purpose. I tapped his cell digits and listened to his end of the phone line ringing.

"Hey!" he answered just before I thought he wouldn't pick up. "Can you and Cheyenne join us at the farm? We're setting up a photo shoot for our website." His voice was excited, and it aided the increase in my uplifting mood. "New puppy owners of Justice Breeders are being featured, and *you* happen to fit that description! Another client called this morning and won't be photographed, so we're short on puppies and owners. Can *you* be here?"

I did a one eighty on the sidewalk and gently tugged on Cheyenne's leash, encouraging her to do the same. Instinctively, she redirected their sniffing and took steps back towards our house.

"I would love to help! But are you sure you don't want to hold out for a real customer? I feel guilty participating because I was gifted my Justice Puppy," I felt myself babbling, but nerves took over when I pictured myself being featured on a public website. "Can just Cheyenne be in the photos? I am not really prepared for being in front of a camera."

"I love your humility, Anna," his voice was sincere and made my heart rate quicken just a bit. "Just come as you are, and we'll snap a few candids. Nothing will be posted without your approval."

I scooped Cheyenne into my arms and attempted jogging back to my house. Her weight seemed to double every fifth step. I set her back down and pulled delicately on her leash with very little success at getting her paws to move faster. Why is it puppies know instinctively what you want, but do the opposite? By the time I could finally make it to the farm, Josh would probably have no use for us. My desire to be with Josh kept me moving, however. Forty minutes later I was unloading Cheyenne's pet taxi from the back of my Jeep. I had taken only time enough to pull my curls into a ponytail and change into my favorite jeans. The rest of my appearance remained as is, per Josh's request.

His charming voice greeted me as he jogged towards my parking spot on the gravel road, "Hey there, you made it!" Josh assisted me in lowering the crate to the ground, and unlatched Cheyenne's door, allowing her to exit freely. It was Cheyenne's first return to the farm since her arrival at my house on Christmas. Her curious nose took to the ground immediately, sniffing a path toward the small crowd of people mingling around the barn. I had not removed her leash after our abbreviated morning walk, so it trailed her as she made her way to the gathering.

Josh smiled brightly at me but turned to catch up with Cheyenne. It took just three lengthy strides and he snatched down for her leash, stopping her mid sniff. I ambled along behind, suddenly feeling reserved about who would be watching this photo shoot.

Josh knowingly sensed my tension. He grabbed my hand with his free hand and pulled me in step with Cheyenne, so we formed a parade of three and marched forward.

"I really appreciate you coming out here so quickly *and* on such short notice. As you can see, we only have four other puppy/owner combinations here today. Not a stellar showing for our website, considering the total number of puppies we've placed in homes," he explained as we neared the barn. Mr. Justice was among the crowd and nudged his wife to look our direction when he saw us. She turned and greeted me with a smile identical to Josh's. She abandoned her conversation and met us on the sidewalk.

"Anna and Cheyenne!" her affable voice gave me the reassurance I needed. My confidence returned without hesitation.

"Good morning, Mrs. Justice, I hope it is okay Josh invited me today," I said, hoping she already knew I was coming. "I don't want to be in the way."

"You are doing us a huge favor being here!" She knelt down and rubbed Cheyenne's chin. "We would love for you to fill in for a customer who bailed earlier this morning. Our website really needs faces of happy dog owners and of course adorable dogs. You and Cheyenne certainly fit that description!" She looked up at me still smiling, waiting for a response.

Cheyenne and Josh looked at me too, and I could only respond with a smile. Being in their presence was comforting and fun. I knew it was going to be a special day.

Logging into the photographer's website later with the password, "puppy love" I was rewarded with dozens of cute pictures. Scrolling through familiar faces of other puppy owners I had met earlier this afternoon; I finally found the small collection of Cheyenne. She was, in my opinion, the most attractive of the furry crew. Feeling fortunate she was mine; I admired our photos. Even the ones I was in did not bother me. Cheyenne was the focal point. I heard the photographer say multiple times it was an ideal day for the shoot. Cloudy and minimal breeze. I clicked the heart on all seventeen of our pictures, saving them as favorites. I typed a quick message to Josh.

Thank you for including us in your project today. I'm looking at the pics now <3

I closed my laptop, set my phone on top, and surveyed my room. It was in desperate need of a major cleaning. Occasionally cleaning seemed like a relaxing activity. Checking the time, I told myself to finish by nine, spend some time with Dad, and be in bed by eleven. I turned on a playlist that reminded me of Wyoming, lit a candle, and got busy. I stripped my bed, sorted clothes littering the floor, organized my dresser, and collected trash. My phone dinged Josh's reply.

YOU saved the day. It was fun!

Smiling, I carried my hamper down to the laundry room and switched clothes from the washer to the dryer. Cheyenne was snoozing in her open kennel, so I crept out, allowing her to continue resting. I grabbed a snack and two trash bags from the kitchen knowing I could easily fill both. Taking the steps two at a time, I reentered my room and was already satisfied with my progress. Another thirty minutes and I would be finished ahead of my nine o'clock goal. I conquered my closet next, humming along to the music. After hanging up clean clothes and finding homes for reunited pairs of shoes, I spent a few minutes dusting with a shirt I dampened in the bathroom. Tossing it in the empty bathroom hamper, I dumped the bathroom trash into the second trash bag. Cleaning the bathroom took longer than organizing my closet but was more satisfying. Mission complete: clean room *and* bathroom and it was only 8:45. I tied the bags and carried them downstairs in one hand. They were full but light, mostly paper and snack wrappers. I checked the kitchen trashcan to see if it was full enough to be carried out to the garage and was disappointed to see two empty wine bottles on top of the trash. I pulled the plastic ties together and lifted the bag. Taking all three bags to the garage can, a conversation with my dad was formulating in my mind. How does one approach a grieving widower regarding his new drinking habits? Simple answer: I don't. Syd does. I went back upstairs to find my phone.

Where are you? I think dad drank two bottles of wine tonight. He's in his room now with the tv on and door closed. I'm worried.

I sent this message to Syd. Was I overreacting? His reply came quickly but did not reassure my nerves.

Marcus and I are having dinner on The Hill. We just got our table. Home by 11. I will check on him when I get there.

Dad didn't need to be checked on. He needed to be challenged. I stole back upstairs noiselessly. Ignoring the clean room that had just been my project, I turned off the lights and music, but left the candle glowing. My bedding was still in the wash, so I found a blanket and wrapped myself comfortably, keeping my hands free. Grasping my phone and pressing it close to my chest, I prayed silently. *Mom, I need help.* Could I will her to text me? Seconds then minutes passed. No reply. Hoping my worry was fallible, I tried remembering my Dad's moods over the last few months. His grief had been teary, but never angry. He kept himself busy with work and helping me with Cheyenne. Alcohol seemed to be a self-destructive choice. I could not bear to watch his pain transpire into something dangerous. I was desperate for help. As I agonized, sleep overtook my thoughts. However, the quality of sleep was marginal. Several dreams coalesced into a nightmare of sorts containing a puppy, a dried-up lake, Dad's shoes, and a dirty blanket. I woke up sweating tangled in my blanket. Still dark outside, I searched my bed for my phone to check the time. Locating my cell on the floor, I freed myself, rolled out of bed landing on my knees, and pressed the home button.

Be strong. Be present.

There it was. The message I so desperately longed for just hours ago. I must have slept through the notification.

Feeling agitated for having missed Mom's message, but also optimistic for her advice, I returned a message.

I need to say something to stop his drinking.

An instant reply.

It is serving a purpose for him right now. He needs a replacement. When was the last time you three went to Mass?

Shame crept into my head. Of course, I attended Mass during my school day, but Dad, Syd, and I had rarely gone since last fall. Maybe only once since Christmas.

Her guidance seemed simple, but effective. Effective, but complicated. Why all of a sudden would I expect him to start going to church again? He would likely be suspicious that I had an agenda.

I checked the time. It was a quarter after six. Still dark outside. Almost twenty-four hours ago I had been sitting at the kitchen table discussing the birthday I wanted to ignore. Then the day spent with Josh and Cheyenne at their farm. That was Saturday. And Saturday came to a close with the discovery of the empty bottles. Now it was Sunday. A new day. A day to give dad a new purpose. A challenge.

I showered and put on a pale sweater. A color hinting that spring and my unwanted birthday were both approaching. I walked down the stairs with heavy steps hoping to wake my dad if he was not already up. The kitchen was empty, however, so I continued with noisy attempts.

Cheyenne was standing in her kennel staring at me curiously as I made my way in her direction. I wished she would start barking. I unlocked her kennel and left the door open wide, giving her the freedom to exit. She walked out slowly and stretched in downward dog. Her routine was the same every time she stepped out. Waiting until she gave her normal shake, I fastened her collar and then attaching her leash, we headed out the garage door. The street was still. No one around here got up before eight on a Sunday morning. I let Cheyenne sniff around every bush and tree in our small front yard before guiding her back inside, letting the door slam loudly as we reentered.

"You're up early," I heard a hoarse voice say from the kitchen. Stepping through Cheyenne's tiled area, I moved cautiously toward my dad. The cynical thoughts in my head were reinforced when I observed the pale and tired look about him. He looked like he had consumed two bottles of wine. Maneuvering around the kitchen a pace comparable to a tortoise, he started a pot of coffee and held up a loaf of bread, offering to make me toast. Remembering to respond to his first statement, I finally spoke.

"There is a nine o'clock Mass at St. Mark's. So, I

will eat later." I sat down at the kitchen table, thinking about Mom's advice. Be present. "Can you take Cheyenne outside while I'm gone?" I looked in her direction as I spoke. She made eye contact with me when I said her name and tilted her head to the side. Smart dog.

Dad remained silent, so I turned back to him, wanting to read his expression. He was contemplating my news, so I added quickly, but casually, "Or I could ask Syd to take care of Cheyenne if you want to go with me." We were both motionless while dad put thought into answering.

"I've been to St. Mark's seven times," he looked at the floor while he spoke. "First, when your mom and I toured the school when we registered you," he looked up. "Then three Sunday Masses in a row right when we moved to St. Louis." Dad sat down across from me and continued his counting, "And then her visitation, and then her funeral, and the last Mass was on Christmas Eve." He stared at me unblinking. I had no idea what was stirring in his mind and failed to create a response. I had not been counting the number of times I had been, but I did avoid sitting where dad and I sat the day of the funeral. I always chose the opposite side, and at the very least, a dozen rows back.

"I could go online and find a ten o'clock Mass downtown?" I asked, hoping the simple factor of geography could solve the issue of getting him to go. "I've been wanting to check out the Basilica."

Dad continued preparing his toast with his back

turned toward me. He took his time buttering several slices, placing them in the toaster oven, and meticulously returning everything to its proper home. Pouring his coffee and taking a seat across from me, he finally answered.

"Go ahead and stick to your nine o'clock plan," he spoke to his mug more than to me. "I have some work to do today on my laptop. Should be finished within a couple of hours." He looked up then, and must have read my disappointment because he added, "I will take Cheyenne for a walk in a bit. And let's go out for lunch." His kind words seemed fabricated, but I appreciated his gesture. However, attending Mass with me would have been a bigger triumph.

I stood up to retrieve his toast before it burned. Placing it in a neat pile, slice on top of slice, I delivered it to the table. I kissed my own fingertips and patted him gently on the crown of his head. Smiling as sincerely as possible, I grabbed my keys from the hook, petted Cheyenne, and walked towards the garage. I could be present, but I couldn't find the words to be a counselor this early in the morning. I would try again later.

As I pulled out of the garage, my phone alerted me of an incoming text. Assuming it was my dad, maybe reconsidering going with me, I flipped it over quickly to see not Dad, but Josh had messaged me.

Want to go to lunch after church today?

Lunch with Josh. The answer was a definite yes, but I couldn't forget my prior invitation from Dad.

My dad mentioned lunch out today too. Can we all three go?

I drove a few minutes before Josh replied. Waiting to reach an intersection with a stop sign, I read,

No need for me to be a third wheel! You two go enjoy the afternoon. We'll do it another time.

Knowing Josh was being polite, I replied back with an offer he couldn't refuse.

I was thinking cheyenne needed her fur trimmed. What if we took you to lunch then you helped me find a local groomer?

His simple reply made me smile.

Deal.

Lunch turned out to be tacos from a local food truck, Cha Cha Chow, just a few blocks from home. Dad and I sat on a bench while Josh sat cross legged on the dry sidewalk. The day was warm, and the sun made its first appearance in several days. The tacos were amazing but enjoying a spontaneous picnic in the sun with these two made me so cheerful I was smiling while chewing.

"Anna, what are you thinking about," my Dad said with his mouth so full it was hard to understand his words. I proceeded to chew and swallow before answering.

"It feels good to be outside eating," I replied. I glanced at Josh, hoping he didn't think I was foolish, and wishing dad hadn't observed my delight. "The seasons seem different here compared to Cheyenne. I don't remember having warm days like this in Wyoming before spring." I took another bite to shut myself up, afraid I was rambling.

Josh's reply was comforting, lacking judgement, "March in Missouri can feel like any season. One year when Easter was in March we bundled up in coats and gloves and built a snow bunny in the fresh snow that had fallen the night before. A couple of years later we ran around barefoot during the annual Justice Family Easter Egg hunt. That's what's great about Missouri. If you don't like the weather, it doesn't matter, it will change fast." Josh finished this description and shoved the remaining half taco into his mouth. Then added while still chewing, "Are you going to finish that last taco?"

Dad chuckled as I handed Josh my leftovers. "You two remind me a little of Eleanora and I when we started dating."

Josh smiled mischievously stating, "Eleanora wasted food too? Anna doesn't eat enough, so I am often forced to offer to eat hers. Seems silly to throw it away."

My Dad wiped his mouth on a napkin and responded comically, "Eleanora ate like a bird. She was always a cheap date." Then patting his stomach added, "I was forced to eat her leftovers and have this to show for it."

Their banter stimulated a sadness that was always just below my surface, even when I was feeling cheerful.

I was becoming more attached to Josh as the weeks had turned into months. The friendship he offered my father was a satisfying addition to his many amazing attributes.

As their conversation continued, I learned something about my mother I had not known. Dad was describing one of their first dates when he broke into a wide smile and declared, "Eleanora even saved a friend's life one time!" I caught my breath at this statement, desperate to know what he knew, and curious why this story had been neglected.

"A small group of us were eating at a local pizza place," Dad said, looking then to me. "You remember Pal's Pizza, right, Anna? That's where we were." He turned back to Josh, "Anyway, we were having fun, probably laughing too much while eating, and my friend, Curt, started choking." Dad paused momentarily, almost reverently, and then continued. "Eleanora performed the Heimlich on him, but he was much bigger than her, so she was unsuccessful." Pausing again, dad looked at me with misty eyes. "Curt finally stopped breathing. Eleanora started CPR while the rest of us looked on helplessly."

I *did* remember that restaurant. It was a local favorite where my Wyoming friends and I went many times after obtaining our licenses and earning the independence that went with it. I was dumbfounded. How could I sit and eat pizza, laugh with friends, do typical teenage things under the same roof that my mother used to do the same, *and* save a life? My palms began sweating as a paralyzed feeling of tension, but also pride overtook me. Why had my mother failed to share with me this incident?"

"Then what?" I heard myself say. I was staring at dad wishing he would talk faster. I needed to know more. Josh had moved closer to me, listening intently as well, and squeezing my sweaty hand.

"The details seem fuzzy now," Dad recounted. "I remember someone took over for Eleanora right about the time Curt started coughing and breathing." Dad stood up as if to signal he did not want to reminisce any further. But then added, "Eleanora saved him, and she got credit for it." He smiled finally and ended with, "Of course she was too humble to enjoy her glory."

We were all three quiet for a couple of minutes as we each processed the story and absorbed the afternoon sun. I finally stood, pulling Josh up beside me. Our trash was collected into one small bag that I tossed into a trashcan. "Let's go get Chey and find a good fur cutter," I suggested, wanting a change of scenery.

Curling up in bed under my favorite blanket, the events of the day scrolled through my mind. Little progress with dad, lunch outside, groomer's with Josh, another amazing dinner by Syd, and studying with some girls from Spanish class. Sitting with dad at lunch seemed like three days ago, not nine hours.

The pleasant sound of my Mom's text alert pierced my thoughts and nudged my heart.

Hey, Tiddlywinks.

Hoping for an answer, I typed my question…

Why didn't you ever tell me about your friend, curt?

Her reply was quick, as if her words existed before my question was asked.

Life and death run in parallel lines. Curt was in the middle, balancing on a third line. He could have fallen either way.

This answer painted itself in my imagination. She was protecting her friend during *and* after his near-death experience. My Mother's humility overpowered her other strengths, even when *she* passed those parallel lines.

I am proud of you. Dad is too, still.

9 EIGHTEEN

The dreaded birthday presented itself with clear blue skies and brilliant sunshine that greeted me through open blinds. March twenty-seventh in Wyoming was typically in the forties. Grabbing my phone from the floor, I checked the forecast and discovered the high today in the St. Louis area was predicted at fifty-eight. Throwing back the covers, I decided promptly to get this day started. Technically, I was born in the evening, so I actually had most of the day to linger as a seventeen-year-old. This year God had gifted me with a Saturday birthday. Thankfully, I could spend the day as I pleased rather than in a classroom.

Downstairs on the kitchen table I discovered a pink rose standing tall in a vase next to a pink envelope. Smiling, but abandoning the idea of gifts, I wandered around the silent house searching for Dad or Syd. Cheyenne was still asleep in her kennel, twisted and upside down as usual. Her lack of being ladylike was of constant humor to me.

Looking for our family's cars and checking my phone for a missed text from either my dad or uncle, I found nothing. Maybe they were taking advantage of the warm morning to work at the concrete plant. They had informed me when the weather improved the business would run on Saturdays.

Returning to the kitchen to admire the pink rose, my phone pinged a new message.

Happy birthday anna marie cabel! I will be back quick just running a little birthday errand. Can I treat you to a latte today?

Well it was my birthday...

Yes skinny vanilla please. Thank you, dad!

I hit send and smiled broadly. Sunshine, latte, no school. My pessimistic attitude was fading. I could handle this day like any other.

I made myself busy in the kitchen to occupy time until dad returned. I found ingredients to make French toast, my very favorite breakfast entrée. I took time to measure the milk, and properly whisk the eggs. In just minutes a wonderful aroma of butter and sweetness filled the kitchen. The scent, or my presence in his kitchen conjured Syd into appearing.

"Birthday girls don't cook, birthday girls relax," my uncle announced as he entered through the garage door. He was carrying a duffel bag I did not recognize that he swiftly slid around the corner into the dining room out of my view. Dismissing this action, I turned and went about my task at the griddle.

"I'm making your famous French toast, but it might be more of the infamous flavor," I offered, hoping he might take over and improve my birthday feast. Trying to appear pathetic I added a fake pout.

"Did you add vanilla?" he asked, "Everyone knows it's just toast if you leave out vanilla." Syd put his phone on the table, purposefully setting it upside down, and covering it with his jacket. He then marched over to my workplace and grabbed the spatula. "Well, you've already started cooking slices, so it's too late to add vanilla," he started to explain. His phone vibrated, and I know he heard, but he made no attempt to retrieve it from hiding.

"I used cinnamon, not vanilla," I began, but then added, "isn't that what Grandma added to her French toast?" Not waiting for an answer, I walked in the direction of his jacket and phone and said, "Where is dad, and where were you?" Knowing it was my birthday, I was not concerned, just curious what both Syd and my dad were hiding. Before he could answer, however, my phone pinged.

Good morning birthday girl! Are you up yet?

Josh was up early for a Saturday. I replied back with voice to text so Syd could hear my side of our conversation.

Thank you and yes I am awake! Syd is making me French toast. Do you want some?

Syd eyed me with a mischievous grin. I could read his mind. He knew that I knew food would lure Josh to our house.

I'm actually on my way to your house.

Oh! Lucky, I had gotten up *and* looked presentable. I was not expecting visitors this early. Voice to text again,

Well hurry it up then! Syd will have breakfast ready soon!
Adding a smiley face with heart eyes, I didn't want to sound too bossy.

"He's on his way here," I informed Syd as I sat down in front of my rose. I picked up the envelope and traced the sealed edge with my forefinger. Turning it back over, I admired my dad's handwriting. He always wrote in all printed capitals. My name stood very lonely though. Mom always addressed cards to me with my middle name included.

"I know," Syd interrupted my thoughts with this news.

I looked up at him as he set the table. He had a stack of five plates in hand. "Ok, I know it's my birthday, but *what?*" I struggled for what exactly to ask. I was very confused. "Where is dad?" I finally asked. And then a string of questions purged, "How did you know Josh was headed here, why five plates, why are you ignoring your calls, and why did you put a duffel bag in there?" I rattled, pointing to the dining room.

Syd ignored my interrogation, focusing on finishing at the table, he was smiling ear to ear. "Birthday girls relax I said," he repeated, looking me in the eyes then. Our eye contact was locked momentarily until Cheyenne's bark suddenly broke in.   I turned to the window, conditioned to expect a visitor upon hearing her yaps.

Not one, but two vehicles pulled up simultaneously. Dad first then Josh's truck parked by the curb. Now my questions would find answers.

I darted out of the kitchen, through the living room, and unlocked the front door. The sight that welcomed me was more than a birthday gift. I ran out of the house barefoot to meet Alexandra, who had dropped luggage and was sprinting open-armed toward me. We embraced in a hug swathed in a mixture of laughter and tears. I surrendered to the emotion of this reunion, and let my crying outlast the laughing. Alexandra finally pulled away, but reached for my hair, pushing it over my shoulders. She used her sleeve to wipe the happy mess from my face. Then drying her own cheeks, finally spoke, "Happy birthday, Anna!" Her voice cracked as another sob escaped.

"You're in Missouri," I let out breathlessly, as if I'd just completed a footrace. "How did…" I stopped, turning to my dad who I knew was standing close by. Transferring my emotions to him, I took seven steps in his direction and offered him a teary hug of thanksgiving. "I cannot believe you pulled this off, Dad," I managed to pronounce. "Thank you. This is an extraordinary gift," I said. Releasing him I turned back to Alexandra who was looking back and forth between Josh and myself.

"I bet you're Josh," Alexandra announced, moving forward with an outstretched hand. Josh stuck out his own hand and they shook, both wearing incredible smiles. A third round of tears emerged, as I wrapped my arms around both of them in a bear hug. My heart was full, and I was reminded of the childhood sentiment of how exhilarating birthdays felt when everything is especially for you. Here I stood in the warmth of Alexandra *and* Josh.

"French toast is ready," Syd sang as he held open the front door, an invitation to move our gathering inside. Dad picked up the dropped luggage, and I grabbed the hands of my two best friends, guiding them up the short flight of porch steps.

As we passed Syd, however, Alexandra wiggled free from my grasp to hug Syd. "We were in such a hurry this morning at the airport, I didn't get a proper hug," she said.

He squeezed her back with one arm, intercepting me with the other. "Bring it in," he returned, "I love these two beautiful faces," and kissed us each on our foreheads. "Even better together."

Finishing our French toast and sipping lattes, I was content just sitting at the table. It was fun listening to them describe the details it took to get Alexandra to Missouri. Between flights arriving late and two cars needed for curbside pick-up, it was a miracle I hadn't figured it out. I guiltily thought if my best friend traveled all this way to Missouri, she most likely did not want to sit in the kitchen for hours. "So, it's Saturday and the weather seems nice," I informed everyone. "We should go do something outside." I looked from Alex to Josh.

"Go to the zoo?" I suggested with a slight chuckle.

Josh smiled, offering instead, "Sounds interesting, but birthday gifts are in order before plans can be made." He retrieved an envelope from an inside pocket of his jacket. He set it flat on the table and gently pushed it towards me with his fingertips.

Dad placed his pink envelope on top of Josh's and added, "We coordinated gifts again. I hope you don't mind conspiracy."

Smiling brightly, but blushing as well, I said, "I'm guessing not another puppy?" Reaching for both sealed envelopes, I opted to open Dad's first. After reading his message I discovered the enclosed certificate was for a local restaurant called Caleco's in downtown St. Louis. I had never heard of Caleco's but assumed Josh must have suggested it. "Thank you, Dad," I stood to hug him then added, "Is Caleco's a lunch or dinner favorite?" Mentally mapping our day, I was discovering Dad and Josh already had plans set.

Josh answered for my dad, "Their menu is broad, anything from steak to quesadillas to pasta. We should go for lunch, right after we go up in the Arch." He turned to Alex then and asked politely, "You're not afraid of heights, right?"

Alexandra laughed boldly, "No, I'm good. I've survived a few ski lifts up on Teton Mountain." She added though, with slight hesitation, "I've seen pictures of the Gateway Arch. Please tell me an elevator delivers us to the top and we don't have to climb like eighty-eight flights of stairs."

That thought had never occurred to me. I had
seen the tiny windows at the top of the Arch, but never
considered how to reach them. I did know it was the
tallest manmade monument in the United States.

Answering again, Josh replied, "Yes, it's a tram
ride, just like an elevator. The Arch Park was recently
renovated. I haven't been through the new museum yet."
Looking at me he added, "I wasn't sure if a museum tour
would be suitable for a birthday activity. I did preorder
tram tickets online because they sell out early in the day."

"I get to spend a Saturday with you and Alex," I
reminded Josh, "Anything we do will be enjoyable!" I sat
back down and picked up Josh's envelope. "I am very
curious," I admitted out loud, "Where else are we going
today?" Tearing into the heavy envelope I expected
another activity to reveal itself. His handwritten message
made me laugh.

*Happy birthday to an amazing girl who was born on the
best day of the year! You were made to be a Missourian!*

"What does this even mean?" I asked. "Made to
be a Missourian?" Josh said nothing, so I opened the
second smaller envelope and pulled out three tickets for a
St. Louis Cardinals baseball game.

"You're celebrating your birthday the same day
our city celebrates the Cardinal's home opener!" Josh
exclaimed. "I know you're not a Cardinal fan, *yet,* but
spend one afternoon in Busch Stadium and I dare you not

to bleed red!" His excitement was contagious. I could care less about professional baseball, but the look on his face was priceless. His love for this team was obvious. How could I *not* want to go?

"We've never been to a professional baseball game, right, Alex?" I looked at Alexandra who was all smiles. She had always loved experiencing new things. This was just one more adventure she could add to her long list.

"I'm in!" she affirmed. "Syd actually filled me in on our itinerary, so I knew this was in the works." Alexandra stood then and searched around for something. "Where's the bag, Syd?"

Syd stood and removed himself from the kitchen returning in seconds with that duffel bag I did not recognize earlier this morning. "You have to dress the part if you're going to be a Cardinals fan," he said, dropping the bag at my feet. Unzipping it revealed a pile of red shirts, jackets, and hats, all bearing the Cardinals famous birds on the bat logo. "Happy birthday from Alex and me," winking at Alexandra he added, "We had fun shopping online and laughing about how many times we picked out identical pieces."

"Which confirms I do have a sense of style, even if we are talking about fanwear and not the latest trends," Alexandra chimed in. "There is also a Jayhawks sweatshirt," she continued and dug through the layers of apparel to find and pull out an oversized blue sweatshirt bearing the KU fathead. "We need to talk about college while I'm here by the way," she said. I got my acceptance letter many weeks ago, and I need a roommate." Alexandra sat back down and stared at me in obvious anticipation. I could feel heat forming in my cheeks as all four of them stared at me. I had completed the online application twice, but never clicked on the submit button. Leaving Dad in St. Louis while I trotted to college had seemed as unbearable as turning eighteen. I did not want my pessimistic thoughts to interrupt today's agenda.

"I completed the application," I offered. Hugging the sweatshirt to my chest, I smiled as a truce, hoping I would not have to explain further.

Feeling sensational with my new white Cardinals tee, ripped jeans, and red ball cap holding my ponytail in place, we loaded my Jeep after Syd and Dad removed the top. I hadn't taken it off since the move to Missouri. I wasn't sure where Dad planned on storing it, but it would need to go back on soon. I was positive weather this perfect in March would definitely be short lived.

"Josh, you should drive," I suggested, knowing downtown St. Louis on a game day was certain to be a challenge. "You know where you're going and where to park." I tossed him my keys which he caught with one hand.

Looking both confident and excited, he returned, "I would love to escort two lovely ladies to their first Cardinal Nation experience." He opened the passenger side door and bowed at the waist adding, "Your chariot for the day, madams."

Alexandra climbed in first and settled herself in the back. A broad smile crept easily across her face as she asked, "Josh, do you have any older brothers?" Her eyes turned to me then and said, "He's such a gentleman. I have never witnessed this level of genuine kindness in our teenage species."

Laughing at Alexandra's compliment, Josh answered, "Unfortunately, all of my siblings have fur and four legs." She attempted to turn her smile into a pout but was unsuccessful. Josh remained standing in the driveway waiting for me to board the Jeep. "Are you ready to get this birthday party rolling?" Without replying, I jogged toward the front porch where Dad and Syd were still struggling with the Jeep top. They stopped as I approached, both knowing I was expecting a hug.

"Thank you for absolutely *the best* gift ever," I told them as we embraced. "I already know I will never forget this birthday." They squeezed me tight and Dad kissed my forehead.

"Go enjoy being eighteen," Dad said, and I thought to myself, *I already am.*

Time was passing too quickly. The Arch visit was more interesting than I had expected. The view from the top was breathtaking. As we peered through the tiny windows to the vast world below, I could feel movement from the wind. It was terrifying, but none of us wanted to venture back down the tram. We gazed and talked for over an hour. Other visitors stayed only minutes. No one seemed to mind we were occupying three windows to ourselves. It was surprisingly spacious at the top of the Arch.

Making our way down and back into the sunshine, we blinked as our eyes adjusted to the brightness. Josh put sunglasses on and informed us the Jeep was parked for the day. We would reach all our destinations by foot.

"Next stop is Caleco's, but we need to take a scenic route to get there. I want you to see City Museum," Josh said as he walked backwards in front of us like a professional tour guide. I expected him to say next, "On your right you will find…" but instead he turned around and walked beside me, reaching for my hand as we strolled.

"Why do you want us to *see* a museum?" Alexandra questioned. Her constant curiosity was always a great source for conversation. "Aren't all the exhibits on the inside?"

Josh answered, "City Museum is not your typical museum." His voice rang with pride, as if he wanted to show off this grand discovery, "It is not what you can *see* inside, it's what you can *do*. *And* how it was constructed. The building itself is artwork."

We walked and talked for several more blocks. Surrounded by skyscrapers and large office buildings we could only see blue sky directly overhead. Finally,

turning a corner, Josh pointed, saying, "There. Look."
Our eyes all shot upward to the top of what I imagined to
be the oldest building downtown. Several stories high
and made of brick, City Museum was a sight. A bus
perched on top looked as if it were about to drive right off
and plummet to its end. An amusement park of sorts also
crowned the building, enticing anyone to come to the top
and ride. "The artists who designed this museum used
recycled pieces to create a unique experience," Josh
explained.

We continued moving toward the museum. Josh
was right, it was fascinating. I almost wished we were
going there instead of the ball game. Then considering
another day trip to the city, I offered, "We need to go
there soon! Now you have me curious to see inside!" I
stopped abruptly to snap a picture with my phone of the
bus dangling off the rooftop. "How did they get that bus
up there?"

Josh stopped too while I took the picture, but
speaking more to Alexandra he replied, "They're open on
Sundays, so we could come back tomorrow. But isn't
your flight back to Wyoming at three o'clock? You really
need several hours to enjoy the museum."

"Right. Three, but I need to be there about one
o'clock to get through security" Alexandra answered. "St.
Louis has a lot to offer. I guess I'll just have to come
back." She took out her phone and handed it to Josh.
"Take our picture in front of this place. I need hard
evidence to take back with me to prove Missouri is pretty
awesome." She pulled me to her side and we both smiled

for the camera. I wanted a picture to capture every moment of this glorious day.

      Waking abruptly the next morning, I checked my phone immediately for the time. Seven-thirty. I had less than seven hours to be with my best friend before she departed for Wyoming, but I didn't want to wake her just yet. I could see she was still sleeping soundly across the room on my loveseat by the set of her jaw and her slow breathing. I closed my eyes again, not really wanting to be awake myself. Replaying yesterday's events in my mind in order from Alexandra's surprise arrival, to eating Ted Drewes Frozen Custard at midnight. The birthday had been perfect, and I didn't want the memories to fade. I was mindful of taking pictures throughout the afternoon and evening. Asking Josh and Alex both to help with this task meant I had a variety of snapshots of us paired off and of all three taking selfies. I had definitely taken more selfies yesterday than in my whole smart phone career. Rolling over and grabbing my phone again, I swiped through the images slowly. The restaurant had tasty food and a very entertaining waiter named Charlie. When Josh told Charlie it was my birthday, he delivered our ice waters in champagne glasses and insisted we have a toast. We toasted to my birthday of course, but then got carried away toasting everything from the empty saltshakers to the lady dining at another table daring to wear a Chicago Cubs shirt in the heart of Cardinal Nation. After laughing and eating for over an hour, we finally made our way to Busch Stadium. Josh insisted on arriving early to earn the opening day bobblehead. "Only the first *twenty thousand* through the gate get one," he said. Thinking our chances were pretty good that we would get a bobblehead, I was amazed to find out we were late. Busch Stadium was almost at capacity at over forty thousand fans. Josh's disappointment didn't last long. He was too busy guiding us to the Coca-Cola Rooftop Patio. "We will be right above the batter's eye. We can see everything!" Josh lead us through the throng, holding tight to my hand. Alexandra stayed close on my opposite side.

When Josh turned, she leaned in and asked only loud enough for me to hear, "What is a batter's eye? It sounds like he's talking about a place, not an actual eye." Her wide curious eyes were silently laughing. She knew we were both clueless regarding baseball.

"Google it when we get to our seats," I told her. "We're probably the only two here who don't know."

More impressive to me was not being above the batter's eye, but directly below the fireworks that erupted both times the Cardinals hit a homerun. I felt the jolt of both explosions in my chest. Absorbing the electric atmosphere of the Stadium was overwhelming. I could easily get used to this and understood why Josh was such an avid fan. The loyalty of the fans was obvious with nearly every seat full on this opening day. All adorned with Cardinal gear. Shirts, hats, jackets, bags, forgotten umbrellas, sunglasses, buttons, belts, even shoes. There was nothing these fans didn't sport to mark them as a Cardinal. And now I was one too. It felt amazing to be part of something so remarkable. Thousands gathered in one massive structure just to cheer for a baseball game. I was in love.

Choosing my three favorite pictures from the day, I posted them to Instagram with the simple caption, "18." It was the first post on my account since last September. I tagged Alexandra and Josh. Hopefully they wouldn't mind. Alexandra's silent phone lit up, notifying her she had been tagged.   And as if on cue, her eyelashes fluttered awake.

"Good morning, Queen of Eighteen," her voice was sleepy, but she looked quite alert. "Can Cheyenne come up to your room?" she asked. "I missed her yesterday when we were out touring your city." She sat up on the loveseat then, searching for something. Finding her phone, she swiped it on and instantly lit up. "Look at us! We look like real baseball fans!" That answered my question of post approval. Thankfully she liked my pictures.

"I will go get Cheyenne from her kennel," I said. "I doubt my dad or Syd have let her out." I fumbled out of bed and took a few steps toward exiting my room when Alexandra noticed my sleepwear.

"You slept in your Jayhawk sweatshirt!" she exclaimed; her words accompanied with a triumphant smile. "I didn't notice you put it on last night."

Looking down absentmindedly, as if I needed to see for myself, I was in fact wearing it, I smiled and replied, "I needed to make sure I looked good in blue and red before committing." I exited my room without waiting for her reaction. I wanted her to absorb that tidbit before we had a full-blown conversation about the reality of being college roommates in just a few months. It seemed so obvious that it was the perfect choice and a smart academic move, but Dad…

I returned within three minutes with Cheyenne and a box of strawberry Pop Tarts. I wasn't hungry but wanted something to offer Alex in case she was. I still felt satisfied from the late-night trip to Ted Drewes. Josh had insisted we experience everything possible St. Louis had to offer in our few short hours together. It was definitely a unique place. With their diverse flavor options, and custard style cream, we ate plenty. Standing around tall tables outside, bathed in the yellow haze of the building's lights, we stayed for at least an hour before feeling like we needed to get out of the way of the crew trying to close. Josh promised he would bring me back with my Dad when I discovered their best-selling custard was called a concrete.

Cheyenne followed me into my room, but abandoned my side to go smell Alexandra, who reached her arms out to welcome her sniffing. She sat cross legged in the center of my room. Cheyenne circled her twice before plopping down in front of her and rolling onto her back, front legs vertical.

"I apologize for her lack of lady like behavior," I warned. It didn't seem to bother Alex, but some motherly instinct made me state this. Noting my dog's social skills was like observing the weather. You could talk about it, but no use trying to change it. Alex rubbed Cheyenne's tummy vigorously and used her best doggy voice to reply, "Snookums just wants attention, that's all, right Chey Chey?" The dog remained in supine position, all four legs now sticking out at odd angles. Then suddenly, as if responding to an unheard alarm, Cheyenne shot up on all fours in one motion, gave a shake nose to tail making her ears flop side to side, and lay back down in a more comfortable, and suitable manner. I took advantage of the moment and snapped a quick picture with my phone, knowing it would be ages before my best friend and my furry friend were both relaxing in my bedroom.

Sunday passed more quickly than my birthday. In an instant we found ourselves at the Southwest terminal, hugging Alex for the last time. More tears emerged as I embraced my friend. Syd and Dad stood a few yards away, giving us some space to talk privately. "Text or call me when you finally make your decision," Alex offered as a farewell. "I completely understand if you choose a local college. But just think, instead of a plane ride apart, we could be sharing a dorm room!" She was increasingly persuasive with her contained excitement. "Your dad seems to be dealing really well," pausing, she glanced back at him then continued, "I know me being here changes your daily dynamic, but he seems stable." Hugging me again, knowing she had pulled a heart string, I took a moment to form my reply.

Finally, I returned, "Let me talk to him. The two of us have avoided the conversation for months. He's a grown man, and I know he will support whatever decision I make," I stopped to look at my dad. He did appear stable. Maybe even content. Turning back to Alex I finished, "I just need to make sure that my decision has his best interests in mind. I don't want to have to move home because he falls apart. Not likely to happen, I know, but my brain cannot help but feel responsible for his well-being. Remember what I told you about his wine consumption. I'm just...worried."

Alex knew my family well. Her last hug was paired with they statement, "Syd's got him. Come to Kansas. Love you."

My sleep that night was restful. In my untroubled dream I was accompanied by Alex, walking a dog in circles around a fountain, looking for something. But I was not certain what we were in search of; answers maybe.

10 APRIL

Sitting in my silent room and looking over my sloppy Spanish notes absentmindedly, I was startled by my phone's trill announcement of an incoming text.

Hi, Tiddlywinks!

She had not texted in days, and for the first time since discovering our paradoxical mode of communication, I wondered in a panic if we would always share this gift. I grabbed my phone.

Mom, will you forever be able to send me messages?

As always, her reply appeared as soon as I hit send.

Only as long as you need my help.

I set my phone on my desk and stared her words. My eyes transferred to the page of notes underneath. I had just conjugated the Spanish verb ayudar, meaning to help or assist. She was helping me but would stop when I was no longer in need of her help. A selfish thought overtook my panic, and I asked...

Can I ask you for help?

Her words came fast.

Like where to go to college?

Of course, she knew what I would ask.

All mothers want control over decisions like that, but it is best decided by the one who holds stake in the effects of choosing. You are eighteen now, remember?

I looked at my notebook again. The Spanish verb listed below ayudar was decidir, to make a decision. My own handwriting was trying to help me make a decision. It *was* my decision. All I needed was encouragement from one more person.

Thanks, Mom. I need to go talk to Syd. Love you!

I crept downstairs wondering if I would be able to catch Syd alone. Away from both Dad and Marcus. Feeling that the stars were in line for me today, I found Syd on the couch joined only by his laptop.

"Can I bug you?" I asked as I made myself comfy right beside him.

He clicked his wireless mouse a few times swiping across his screen before answering, "Only if you rephrase that question because Anna Cabel never bugs me." Closing the laptop, he gave me his full attention.

"Ok," I smiled, "Can I ask for your advice?" I turned sideways so we were facing each other.

"I am not a parent, but I heard some good

parenting advice recently. It was to shut up and listen. So, I'm shutting up and listening. Go." His eyes were bright and friendly. Syd was the most approachable, considerate person I knew, and I valued his unbiased opinion.

I took a deep breath and spit it out, "I want to go to KU and be Alex's roommate. I'm terrified to leave Dad. He'll fall apart without me here. Or he'll drink unnecessarily." It felt good to say the words for someone to hear. Releasing the ideas into the open air in our living room made me feel like I already had conviction of my plan.

Syd remained focused, asking simply, "Do you have an idea of what you might study?"

Surprised he didn't already know that answer, I replied, "Journalism. But I've been on their website a few times and noticed they have a wide range of degree programs. In case I change my mind."

His reply made me laugh, "Are you sure you don't want to attend my alma mater and pursue a degree in management? We could really use more females in our workforce. You know…equal opportunity?"

"I'm positive I do not want to work at the concrete plant, no offense." I leaned in for a hug. "I don't think what I want to study is my issue. It's leaving Dad."

Syd put both of his arms around me, "Anna, you are not leaving your dad, or me. You're just putting a little bit more space between us."

Where had I heard something like that before?

Syd sighed deeply then considered, "You know, Anna, I met Elenora when she was eighteen. You look more like her every day, but maybe even more stunning. The same cheek bones and smile. You have some Cabel in your looks too, though." He continued to analyze my face while he spoke. "Your dad and mom used to take me on their dates even though I was younger. I think I offered support during those first awkward moments when conversation was difficult. Nora called me "her other boyfriend," and often said she felt like she was dating both of us. This never bothered me even though it was about that time I became less interested in girls." A mischievous smile spanned his face, and I tried to imagine my uncle at the age of sixteen.

"Your mom would be so proud of you. I am so sorry I neglect to remind you daily just how remarkable you are. Your mom would have," he finished.

My thoughts shifted to the private conversations I shared with my angel. In her own way she was still encouraging me. Guilt layered itself in my core like geologic bands. A millennium would pass before I would share with Dad or Syd this treasure.

Bringing our focus back to Dad I asked, "Where is Dad?" I peeked over my shoulder as if thinking he might have been standing there silently, listening to our whole exchange.

Syd sensing my instant tension, reassured, "He checked out an hour ago. Wine-free I might add." He closed his laptop and shoved it in the backpack that was his briefcase. "I'm doing the same. This kid needs his beauty sleep. Early day tomorrow." Syd kissed my forehead and left me alone on the couch.

Considering texting Josh, I checked the time. Quarter past eleven. Maybe too late to send a message, but he could just read it in the morning.

All signs are pointing me in the direction of KU. But I'm having a hard time with the finality of my choice. Your thoughts?

Holding my phone momentarily and staring at my sent message, I was surprised to see bubbles appear telling my Josh was typing.

You are asking my advice knowing I'm going to MU? Lol. I'm sure you are aware MU and KU are fierce rivals?

Alexandra had informed me of this when I mentioned to her that Josh had been accepted to the University of Missouri.

Just collecting opinions of all those I care about. I feel like I'm choosing my epitaph, and it can never be changed.

I hit send and immediately regretted my words.

That's an unusual analogy.

I knew that sounded morbid. I tried again.

I do not feel comfortable making a decision that will directly affect my dad. It seems permanent to move to Kansas.

Josh's bubbles came and went. This was going to be a long reply.

You are in a unique situation, so the choice is a hard one. The fact that you are putting so much consideration into your plans shows what kind of a person you are. You are compassionate about your family. That family is just a car ride away. And you'll pass me in Columbia traveling home! Plus, KU has a great journalism program, and I know that's where your heart is.

How does Josh know where my heart is, and I don't?

Thank you. See ya tomorrow in class. Xo

As I walked upstairs to go to bed, Josh's final text came.

And I can't wait to hear what my new college friends say when I tell them I'm dating a Jayhawk!

Maybe because it was late, or maybe because I had made my decision, but my mind was still and dreamless that night. And many nights to follow.

Alexandra took the news well when I informed her, I had been accepted to Kansas University, and needed a roommate.

You just made my day! You just made my year! I love it!

We need to pick out coordinating bedding and decorations for our dorm!

Leave it to Alex to require an interior decorator for a dorm room.

Hold your horses, sister. It's only April. We have until August. More importantly, we need to discuss prom.

Knowing this would distract her, I waited for a speedy reply.

Did josh ask you?!? How did he ask?!? Details!!!

Prom was exactly one month away, and I was confident Josh would invite me. He had been hinting around for weeks, probably trying to decide if I would say yes before going overboard on a fancy proposal.

He hasn't asked yet, but I think he will. I was wondering if I could wear your dress from junior year prom? Shopping sounds depressing.

I could hear confused excitement in her words.

Absolutely! What about Syd? Wont he insist on shopping and dressing you?

She was right about Syd. He would demand some level of participation in prepping me.

I will compromise with syd. He can help with my hair, makeup, jewelry… I am not shopping. I will spend the whole time dwelling on who is not with me. Can I please wear your dress?

Her reply was accompanied with a picture of the two of us a year ago at our Junior Prom. A group of girls went solo. It had been one of my best memories of Wyoming. Alex's dress was full length, a sparkling dull plum color, with thin straps. It looked elegant with her hair color which matched mine almost identically.

The dress is yours. I'll ask my mom to ship it asap. Can't wait to see how gorgeous you are when Syd dolls you up right!

Perfect. I was set with a Prom dress and college roommate. Now all I had to do was anxiously await an actual Prom proposal.

I was pleasantly surprised when that wait took only until the end of the week. Prom was presently off my mind when Josh texted.

We should go check out forest park tonight. Maybe get some more frozen custard?

I replied back simply,

I'm in!

He said he would pick me up close to six. That meant I would be home with Dad and Syd for their Saturday afternoon meal. They had been banking on a warm weekend all week. Syd and Marcus wanted to experiment with the new smoker recently purchased, and Dad was eager to forget work and relax on the back patio.

"I'll be here for the feast. What are we smoking?" I informed them as I walked out of the open door onto our patio. Brightly lit by sunshine, the day was beautiful. As promised by the meteorologist, it was warm with very little breeze. I sat in the last available chair surrounding the table. Syd and Marcus both held drinks in glasses that were condensing puddles on the tiled tabletop. Dad was sipping white wine.

"You're in for a treat, Anna," Syd started. "We're making chipotle molasses ribs, blueberry bourbon ribs, and of course some peppercorn ribs." His dazzling smile was matched by his partner's. Marcus seemed just as excited to share the smoking enthusiasm.

"It will be mouthwatering," Marcus added. "Unfortunately, we have been out here laboring intensively over the meat and will have no sides dishes to offer." Chuckling at his own remark, Syd nodded vigorously.

"I'm not a culinary master like you two, but I can handle a salad, or throw rolls in the oven," I offered. The ribs smelled good, but a pile of just meat for dinner did not sound appetizing. Especially if Josh and I were headed to Ted Drewes Frozen Custard later.

Dad finally chimed in, "That would be great, Anna, I can help you in the kitchen. The ribs probably still have an hour to go." He took another sip of wine while I continued to look at him. Was drinking wine at three in the afternoon necessary?

Before I could put too much thought into my dad's drinking, he informed me a package had arrived earlier. It was by the front door.

"My dress!" I squealed and hopped up from the table. Sprinting through the glass door, through the kitchen, and into the living room took only seconds. I grabbed the box and was instantly unsure if it was the dress because of its weight. Double checking the return address was Wyoming, I was reassured seeing Alex's handwriting. I walked more slowly back to the patio wanting to protect the contents.

"What dress did you order without my approval?" Syd asked in a hurt voice. He stood and walked to my side of the table. Only Syd would be as excited about a dress as I was.

I hugged the box before setting it down. "I didn't *order* a dress, I *borrowed* a dress," I bragged. Marcus had already pulled out his pocketknife and offered it to me. I accepted it, and carefully managed to just puncture the tape with its tip. Opening the box revealed the dress, even more exquisite than I remembered. It sparkled in the sunlight as I lifted it. I heard a sharp intake of breath from Syd, he approved. I held the straps to my shoulders letting the gown drape the length of me. The delicate fabric slightly changed from its dull plum to a shade of blue as I moved.

My dad had to clear his throat before he could speak. "You will be the loveliest girl at the dance," he said softly. I could tell he was holding back tears.

Not wanting to turn this picnic into a sob story, I gently folded the dress into thirds and started placing it back in the box. But before I could, I noticed the silver heels Alexandra had worn with this dress last spring. And with them, a note.

"I'll be upstairs," I said, and quickly packaged the items. I wanted privacy to read Alex's note. I exited quickly before Dad or Syd could ask any questions.

Finding a hanger and securing the dress on my closet door, I took a few steps back to admire its beauty. I removed the heels from the box and set them gently below the hem of the dress. With the letter in hand, I sat myself down, facing my Prom attire. I unfolded the letter and read,

Anna,

You amaze me. I know this year has been difficult with the move and losing your mom. You have handled it with grace. I can only hope to ever have an ounce of your maturity and class. Our friendship has, and always will, be constant. Knowing your strength makes me strong too. I cannot wait to start college life with you. Just like Syd said, we're better together. xoxo Alex

I read her note three times before neatly folding it and placing it in my top dresser drawer. It would rest there with my broken locket and the newer locket from Dad that still did not have pictures in its tiny frames. I slowly closed the drawer. Watching my treasures leave my sight felt like I was bidding them a sort of farewell. I reopened the drawer just as slowly to double check they still existed. Feeling reassured, I closed the drawer more confidently this time and released the knobs. Turning to look for my phone, I jumped when I realized Syd was at my door, staring at my compulsive behavior.

"Sorry, Anna," Syd offered, stepping into my room and moving toward my hanging dress. "I wanted a better look at this gown." He gingerly lifted the hanger with one hand, and took the fabric between his fingertips, judging its quality. "It is lovely. I assume Alex sent you this? I think I remember her in this color last year," he said.

With my phone in hand, I snapped a quick photograph of Syd holding the dress while answering, "Yes, it is from Alex. I'm sending her a picture, so she knows it arrived," I explained. I hit send and turned to face Syd. Still not ready to discuss Prom, I completely shifted gears on him. "Should Dad be drinking at three o'clock in the afternoon?" Waiting for his response, I continued to stare at my uncle.

Chuckling, he replied, "What? You're not worried about Marcus and me day drinking? Just your dad?" He topped his laugh with a genuine grin. "It has been an overwhelming week at the plant. He deserves a break. We're not driving anywhere this evening, if that helps."

I tried to collect my thoughts before responding. "I just want Dad to be safe...and happy. And find a better way to cope," I said. The subtle way Syd dropped his shoulders and the set of his eyes told me he was processing my concern and forming an answer. A solution I hoped.

"Marcus and I have talked about his drinking too," Syd said then added, "We know you're worried." He put his hands on my shoulders and turned me, so we were looking each other square in the eyes. "Marcus thinks your father should seek professional counseling to deal with his grief. Christopher is haunted by more than just the loss of your mother. Moving to Missouri, demands of work, being a single father..." Syd pulled me into a hug and said reassuringly, "I think he's doing well despite the circumstances, but we do need to keep his consumption in check."

Breaking from Syd's embrace, I turned away and offered, "Mom says we need to go to Mass more often." Before the sentence was completely formed in my brain and released to my voice, my face felt flush, and my arms felt weightless. How could I just blurt that out? There were no thoughts in my head except panic. With a pounding heart I looked back at Syd. I felt transparent. He could surely see right to the secret I had kept hidden all these months. Exposing it all by referring to Mom in the present tense. Could Syd perceive my betrayal?

"Going to Mass sounds like a positive," Syd concurred, "Let's go tomorrow morning." He took steps toward my door making an exit but stopped. "I'm sure Father Nicholas would love to meet Marcus," he chuckled then disappeared, leaving me with sweaty palms. I took several deep breaths attempting to calm myself. Revealing the communication, I had shared with Mom would undoubtably make me sound foolish. Syd suspected nothing. An angelic text tone terminated my angst.

Relax.

That one simple word erased my tension.

Thanks, mom. Xoxo

I decided to change clothes and get ready for Josh to pick me up. He wouldn't arrive for over two hours, but if I was ready, I could spend time with Dad in the kitchen preparing our contribution to dinner. I was not sure what to expect at Forest Park, but I did know we would be outside. Choosing old jeans and a comfortable yellow top, I spent more time on my hair. I carefully worked a single plait into a low ponytail and secured it with an extra hair band. Checking my reflection, I concluded Syd was right. I did favor my Mom more than the Cabel side of the family. Feeling sanguine, I went downstairs to enjoy the rest of the afternoon with my favorite family members.

Josh arrived before six, and was ushered in by Syd, who handed him a plate. "Please try all the flavors," he encouraged, as Josh surveyed the ribs still spread on the kitchen table. "We made more than enough!"

I giggled as Josh greedily piled his plate with an enormous helping or ribs. "Were you deprived of lunch and dinner?" I asked, opening the patio door so he would find a seat outside with us. Marcus pulled over an additional chair so we could all five sit around the table.

Josh's quirky confidence made us all laugh when he answered, "My Mom has been feeding us like rabbits. She thinks my Dad needs to lose some pounds, so all she makes are salads. I haven't been fed properly for weeks."

"Men and meat," I muttered. I was satisfied with salad but understood. Cheyenne came out and settled herself comfortably at my feet. Probably hoping I would pass her a nibble. My plate was empty, so I nudged Josh with my foot, and nodded toward the dog. He read my mind accurately and tore a piece of meat off and hand fed her. The five of us sat for most of an hour talking and laughing. In an attempt to wrap up the conversation so Josh and I could leave, I stood and gathered the empty plates. Dad took my cue and carried the glasses. In the kitchen we washed dishes and put away leftovers. Josh followed us, offering to help, but instead I asked him to feed Cheyenne.

"Josh and I are going to Forest Park tonight, Dad. We'll be home before ten or so. Can we go to Mass tomorrow?" I didn't look at him while I spoke. I focused on wiping crumbs from the kitchen table while he took in my invitation.

Dad dried his hands on the dish towel and returned it neatly to the hook. And then without hesitation he offered, "Sounds like a plan. What time are we going?"

An amazing contentment settled inside me, "Let's find a Mass around 9:00, and then go out for a late breakfast?" I suggested. "We don't have to go to St. Mark. We could drive to Kirkwood, or Creve Coeur."

Dad smiled, nodded, and walked back outside to join Syd and Marcus, ending our conversation.

Josh drove to Forest Park with music blaring. We both sang along to familiar classic rock songs playing on his satellite radio. After parking we both walked toward the Boathouse still singing Mellencamp's *Hurts So Good*.

"Have you ever been on paddleboat?" Josh asked reaching for my hand as we crossed the crowded parking lot. "They close the boat rentals in an hour or so, but that gives us time to take a short ride around the park."

"Canoeing, yes, but never a paddleboat," I declared. "I'm guessing they don't take too much skill."

Josh grinned, "Zero skill. Let's get one and start paddling before it's too late!"

We boarded our tiny vessel, and within minutes were making our way on the narrow waterway. For as crowded as the parking lot was, it seemed we had the stream to ourselves.

"So, you're set on KU, right?" Josh asked as he guided our boat away from a fallen log. Two turtles dived off in fear of a collision.

I took a few seconds to consider attending the University of Missouri with Josh. It would be much closer to Dad.

"It's only a few months away, but I am having such a hard time imagining myself as a college student. Too much change. I'm just now getting accustomed to Missouri, and being so far from Wyoming, which I still feel is my home." This time I reached for Josh's hand. I flattened my palm against his, measuring the difference in the lengths of our fingers. His strong hands made me feel safe. I would definitely miss the comfort of our friendship next year.

"To me, the unknown is an opportunity," Josh returned. "The security of home is always a call, or a drive away."

"True. And I like the idea of being busy, making new friends, taking classes that are relevant, but...'" my voice trailed off. "There is this extreme darkness that is eluding my vision of the future. It's as if I spoke with a psychic and her crystal ball showed nothing but gray smoke." I longed for this pessimism to dissolve.

We paddled silently for a minute, floating under a walking bridge. The sky was turning a shade darker. The golden rays were tattooed streaks of lavender clouds, announcing the sunset.

"We can plan and prepare all we want for the future, but we're never in control," Josh said easily. "You have conquered some serious obstacles in your life recently. Look at how positive and compassionate you are. That's what I love about you. Your resilience."

Hearing the word *love* caused my heart's rhythm to speed. I glanced at Josh as he continued his thoughts. He gazed straight ahead while he paddled. "Plus, if you're at KU, you'll have Alex, and she's family. I can tell from the one day I spent with the two of you that you share more than a friendship. Are you sure you weren't twins, separated at birth? The way you can finish each other's sentences..."

Blushing slightly, from his compliments and

knowing that word *love* still hung in the air, I answered, "Yeah, we look similar too. People used to ask if we were twins. It was fun sharing clothes, something I can look forward to, being her roommate this fall." I tried not to smile, thinking about her prom dress secretly hanging in my closet.

"You two can road trip to Columbia and visit me," Josh said. "Alex would probably be up for meeting new people. Lawrence to Columbia is less than a three-hour drive."

Taking a minute to contemplate his scenario, I looked skyward. Tree branches framed my view, but I could see the lavender had faded to a mixture of purples and rose. I wondered selfishly if my Mom had painted this sky for us. I reached for my phone that had been securely stashed in my drawstring bag resting between us. I wanted a picture of this masterpiece. I snapped one and sent it to Dad, and then another and sent it to Josh. His phone vibrated, alerting him of my photo, and he reached for his jacket pocket. Assuming he would withdraw his phone and inspect my photography, I was surprised instead to see a bracelet in his hand.

Turning in his plastic seat to face me, Josh reached for my wrist with his free hand. As he gently pulled my arm, he worked at fastening the delicate leather strands snug around my wrist. Smiling, he said softly, "Read it."

Lifting my wrist for a closer look, I rotated the bracelet to reveal opposite the clasp was a small silver heart tied neatly to the center strand. Knots held it tight on both sides so it would remain in place on top of my arm. The heart had one word inscribed in a beautiful font followed by a question mark.

Prom?

The rhythm of my heart accelerated once again. Josh sat frozen in our paddleboat, staring at me with anticipation. With no feet on our boat's pedals, we drifted aimlessly. Skimming a patch of reeds, we avoided the bank by just inches. Inhaling steadily, there seemed to be a boulder in my throat, preventing me from answering the bracelet's simple question. Happy tears were threatening to emerge if I spoke. Here we sat under a brilliant sky, floating among the cattails and turtles, and Josh so casually dropped that word *love*. My heart decelerated and instantly melted to a puddle of mush.

"Prom?" I said, almost inaudibly, speaking more to my wrist than to Josh.

"Anna, will you please go to Prom with me?" his voice was more hesitant than the confident expression he wore on his face. My reaction must have confused him.

Composing myself, and reorganizing my thoughts, I finally managed to speak more clearly, "Prom would be fun. I would love to go with you," adding a smile to reassure him that my answer was genuine. The tears behind my eyes retreated on their own. The affect Josh was having on me tonight was powerful, but welcome.

Josh touched the heart on my bracelet with his

thumb and he wrapped his fingers under my palm, fitting our hands together perfectly. He tilted his head toward mine, leaving just centimeters between us. I lessened the space by resting my head on his chest and embracing him in a hug. Kissing my forehead, he said in a hushed tone, "Thank you for saying yes. I love you, Anna Marie."

11 PROM

Staring at my reflection, I was mesmerized by the person staring back. She did not look like me at all. Too sophisticated, too much makeup. Syd approved, however. Arguing with Syd would change nothing, so I was resolved to the fact that I looked slightly plastic. Alex's dress and shoes fit perfectly. She had texted throughout the day, begging for a picture. Finally, I sent one, expecting her exact response.

Awww. My baby girl is all grown up. Behave tonight, young lady!

I laughed silently which tightened my chest. My nerves and excitement were taking over. I tossed my phone on my bed and took one last look in the mirror. The late evening sun coming through my open blinds swept across the iridescence of the dress. The slight change of color was fascinating. My hair in long curls hung the length of my back. Syd had pinned up just one thick lock with a stylish clip he said he found when he was shopping downtown. My guess was, he went shopping specifically for that clip, wanting to contribute to my ensemble. It was simple, yet elegant, with diamonds matching my small princess cut earrings. I heard the doorbell, announcing Josh's arrival. He was early, as usual.

Gripping the stair rail with my right hand and lifting my dress away from my heels with my left, I descended the steps carefully. Why hadn't I thought to practice walking in these impossible shoes?

"To say you look beautiful would be inaccurate," I heard Josh say from the bottom of the stairs. I was only making eye contact with my feet in fear I would fall down the remaining steps and ruin our evening. Upon reaching the safety of stable flooring, I finally looked at Josh with a smile. "Exquisite would be a better description," he finished. Raising my left hand with his, Josh kissed it, and slightly bowed as if we were royalty. I then took notice of his attire. Black tuxedo, white vest, white tie. His dark brown eyes were bright with excitement. He too, looked quite lovely.

"How charming," I teased. "You look like a prince headed off in search of Cinderella."

"I guess that makes you Cinderella," he returned. "Does Cinderella want flowers on her wrist this evening?" He produced from behind his back a corsage of white roses and silver ribbon. A nice compliment to my sparkles and silver heels. I had a feeling Syd might have had something to do with how perfectly it coordinated.

Dad entered the living room with his phone in hand. "No escaping until I have a few pictures!" He looked me head to toe then added, "Anna Cabel, you look radiant."

"I will take credit for that!" Syd mused, as he joined us. "And let's go take pictures outside. The clouds out there are overtaking the sunshine. Perfect for photography."

Josh and I lead the way out the front door, down the steps slowly, and into our small lawn. Some trees had early leaves, and many bushes had bloomed. This early in May, though, much of our vegetation still dormant. Syd suggested standing near the bright yellow forsythia bush. He diligently positioned my dress, so it hung to his satisfaction before stepping back to take some pictures.

I felt Josh's gaze on me and turned to face him. "You look a little nervous, don't be. Tonight, will be fun," he whispered for only me to hear.

For whatever reason, I did feel a bit anxious. Maybe it was the borrowed dress I was responsible for. Or going out with a group of Josh's friends I had not spent much time with before. I was trying to keep my expectations very low, so as to not be disappointed if the evening was not enjoyable. I didn't reply to Josh, just simply smiled and took a deep, audible breath. Josh smiled in return and squeezed my hand slightly.

"Ok, kids, I think we're finished here," I heard Syd say.   I had momentarily forgotten we were supposed to be posing for pictures.

"What? I didn't even smile for the camera," I questioned, looking at my uncle.

"I took a couple dozen while you two were

whispering and battling your eyelashes at one another. Promise I got some good shots. No one likes stiff posed pictures anyway." Syd smiled broadly, revealing that award-winning grin. "And Marcus said you can take his Corvette if we can drive your Jeep tonight. Deal?" He reached in his pocket, pulling out keys and tossed them to Josh before we had a chance to process the information.

Josh caught the keys. Wearing a smile to match Syd's, he asked, "Seriously?"

Syd laughed, "Marcus thinks you're good kids," then added with forced authority, "Prove him right."

Josh turned down the volume of the *Hamilton* soundtrack Marcus had blaring on his Corvette's stereo. "Whoa," Josh laughed, "Love me some Lin-Manuel Miranda, but tonight is not the night for Broadway!" He took a minute to pair his own phone to the car then turned the volume back up. I smiled as we drove through my neighborhood listening to Queen's *Don't Stop Me Now.* And of course, Josh knew every. single. word.

Dinner was predictable, but entertaining, nonetheless. We arrived last, so were seated at the end of a long table full of our prom party members. Everyone greeted us with a hello and friendly smile as we took our seats. Across the table from us were Josh's friend, Rory, and his date. I knew Rory well from having had a class with him, but his date, Chloe, was unfamiliar. She had a bright smile and introduced herself immediately. "You must be Anna! I'm Chloe. I go to Mid Rivers High School. I'm tagging along with this clown because he needed a date, and I was free. I love your dress, it must be from Wyoming? I didn't see it in any of the shops here when I was shopping. I would remember that dress!"

I laughed internally at her rambling introduction. Is that what I sounded like sometimes? "Actually, you're right! It is from Wyoming. I stole it from my friend's closet, so hopefully I don't drop my dinner on it. I'm sure she'll want it back." And adding with a smile to match hers, "Yes, sorry, I am Anna."

Throughout our meal the four of us talked and laughed. Josh and Rory kept the conversation lively as they bantered back and forth about sports scores, graduation, college rivals, and local bands. Apparently, Rory and his two older brothers started a band that had played locally at St. Louis bars and street fairs.

"Too bad your band isn't booked as our Prom entertainment tonight," Josh was saying. He turned to me and added, "Every year the upper classmen complain about the music at Prom. You'd think with having a dad for a principal I could have some sort of say in who they hire."

Rory was quick to respond however, "As much fun as it would be to play for our friends, it would kind of take away from my Prom experience." He looked at Chloe then and continued, "I am most looking forward to being the envy of all when I am on the dance floor with my hot date."

Chloe could hardly contain her laughing, "And what if that hot date happens to be a horrible dancer?"

"No worries," Rory said, "I have a secret weapon that guarantees stellar dance moves." He flashed open his tux coat to reveal inside his chest pocket he had a pint of vodka. He grinned and bragged, "Plenty to share!"

I momentarily froze. This was what I was anticipating would happen tonight, just not this early in the evening. My lack of drinking experience left me speechless. Surely Josh was thinking the same thing. And sure enough, his voice came to my rescue, "Dude, keep it covered. You know that's not my scene. My dad would have my ass."

"Right, right," Rory laughed. "More for me and Chloe then." He glanced her way and was rewarded with a knowing smile. She obviously concurred.

Josh squeezed my hand under the table, sensing my tension. Lucky for both of us, the server delivered the bill for dinner, saving us from what could have turned our fun meal into an awkward farewell. Josh grabbed the black sleeve that held the bill and handed it back to the server with a credit card. "Principal Justice will pay for our four meals," he told the server.

"Whoa, no fair, I will pay," Rory objected, but it was too late. The server walked away, distracted by others in our party trying to pay. "Thanks, man, you didn't have to do that."

"Glad to do it. Pay it forward." And with that,

Josh stood, ushering me to do the same. He guided me out of the restaurant with limited small talk and waves to friends still sitting at our long table. We stopped at the servers' station to leave a tip and collect his dad's credit card.

It felt good to be outside in the fresh air. Night had settled, and the short rain had passed, leaving the pavement slick. Josh held my hand as we crossed the parking lot to Marcus's Corvette. Josh had parked as far away as possible in an unoccupied corner of the lot to prevent careless motorists from scratching or denting the doors. Even though he was excited to have this car for the night, I could tell he was nervous to have this responsibility.

"Sorry about Rory. I knew he'd be drinking sometime tonight, but I thought he'd have the decency to keep it a little less conspicuous." Josh opened the door for me, and I carefully adjusted my long dress before climbing into the low seat. He circled the car and got in the driver's side. "I hope he didn't offend you, Anna."

"Oh my gosh, it's no big deal." I struggled to find the right words to explain my feelings. I did not want to sound like a prude. The choices that others made was their business, and I would not pass judgement. However, I was hoping I would not be harassed because I chose not to partake.

"In Cheyenne my friends and I kept busy with other stuff. We weren't in a party crowd, and everybody knew it. I bet classmates talked about us, but we didn't care. We had our own fun." My voice sounded sad as I gave this testimonial. I felt pathetic, so I added, "You don't drink, right?"

Josh turned slowly out of the parking lot and into heavier traffic. I wasn't sure if he didn't answer because he was focused on driving, or he didn't want to tell me that I was a loser for not drinking. A full minute passed before he finally spoke. "I did drink. My freshman year." His eyes looked straight ahead at the road, not even glancing my way. I couldn't even bother blinking as I stared at him, trying to read his expression. "My parents found out from some parents of a junior whose house I was at one weekend. They told my parents they *thought* I had some drinks. I'm sure they were trying to protect themselves, and their son. They knew the party at their house had gotten out of control with teenagers drinking. They knew I was trashed."

We slowed and then stopped at a red light. Josh looked at me. The urgency in his expression told me he needed forgiveness for this act he did three years ago. "Did your parents learn the truth?"

"Yes and no." Josh accelerated when the light was green and put his eyes back on the road. "I had a guilty conscience, so I told them I was drunk at that party. I was in plenty of trouble and was so sick the next day I knew I deserved every ounce of it. I vowed to myself I would not drink again in high school. That is how I justified not telling them that wasn't the first time I drank. But I do know it was the last. I haven't had a sip since." His face looked serious. Despite the time that had passed since this incident, I could tell it still weighed heavily on him.

"Well aren't we a pair," I smiled and pulled one of his hands from the steering wheel. I kissed his knuckles. "I bet your parents forgave you a long time ago." I took a quick deep breath, somehow hoping we could change the subject.

Josh returned a smile just as genuine as mine. "Find some good, *loud* music. We need to make a statement with our entrance in this ride!"

Happy that he was just as eager to dismiss the issue of drinking, and happier there would be no pressure on me to drink tonight, I found the perfect song to prepare us for the dance floor...Prince's *Let's Go Crazy.*

It was a tradition for St. Mark's to host Prom in the ballroom of the downtown Hilton. I had not been downtown since my birthday, so driving these streets flooded my memory of my birthday with Alexandra and Josh. It felt so peculiar to be wearing her dress at a moment I was missing her so much. I took a quick selfie of Josh and I in the Corvette and sent it to her in Snapchat. She must have had her phone in her hand because the reply came immediately.

Look at you! xoxo

Her words made me feel like we weren't quite so far apart. A content feeling overtook my nerves as we walked into the ballroom. It was brilliantly decorated with a dozen massive chandeliers, white tablecloths on high top tables, bouquets of white roses, and made complete with an ice sculpture on an hors d'oeuvres table.

"I think this is the wrong ballroom, this looks like a wedding," I said before looking beyond the decorations and noticing familiar faces.

"No, this is Prom. Last year I didn't go, but I helped set up. I think some parents live vicariously through their kids," Josh laughed and then nodded his head toward a group of adults huddled in a corner. "They're so busy analyzing, they'll forget they're supposed to be chaperoning.

I scoffed, but admired the effort put into detail. "Our Prom last year was in the school gymnasium. It didn't look anything like this. We did have a good DJ though. It was pretty amazing. I remember my feet hurting for a couple of days."

"I dare us to be the first two on the dance floor," Josh challenged, all smiles. The music was loud, and I liked the song playing. Not giving me time to object, Josh took my hand and lead me forward. My tension, grief, and self-consciousness all seemed to disappear as we danced. We were joined within minutes by at least two dozen classmates, and the crowd grew larger with each song. Carrie, Trish, Jen, and their dates joined our circle. They made me feel even more comfortable. I made a mental note to reach out to them more often. They could end up being lifelong friends like Alexandra if I made an effort to be social on a regular basis. For three hours straight we danced, stopping just once to remove my heels and grab a drink.

I decided to check my phone while we were taking a break. I pulled it out of its hiding place in Josh's coat pocket which was hanging on the back of a chair. I had two missed messages. One from Dad,

Have fun tonight! Love you, beautiful girl!

And a second from Chloe,

Meet me in the bathroom if you want to help me finish this bottle!

Why did I give her my cell number? The words sitting on my screen were like an elephant in the room. I showed Josh my screen as he approached our table. His eyes widened and he held back a laugh.

"Don't open it. She'll think you never saw the text." He snatched the phone from my hand and slid it back in its hiding place. With a grin he wrapped his arm around my waist and pulled me towards the crowd just as the music transitioned to a slow song. Josh's hand on my hip cleared my mind of the text. We joined our friends who had all paired off as couples. Josh pulled me in close, leaving no space between us. I rested one palm on his chest, and the other wrapped comfortably over his shoulder. With my heels off I felt myself having to look up to meet his gaze.

"You're having fun," he said knowingly. "What do you want to do when we leave here? We're invited to a post party at the Adair twins' house. There will definitely not be drinking there. Or we can just go home. Totally up to you." His smile was so lovely, and his hands were still resting on my hips. I didn't really want to think about the dance ending. I needed more slow songs. Would he kiss me right here in front of chaperones? "Anna?" I loved hearing him say my name. I was taking too long to answer.

"I don't know. Are Carrie and Trisha and that group invited to the Adair's house?" I guess if the dance had to end, at least I could choose the option that gave me more time with Josh. Instead of just going home.

"Let's ask them." He pulled on me slightly, guiding our slow dance toward Carrie and her date, John. They were next to Trisha and Matthew who spun around elegantly to face us, all while remaining attached to one another. "What are you guys doing after this?" Noticing other couples making out on the dance floor humored me. The six of us were still dancing as couples, but probably appeared to be convening in a business meeting. "We're debating Adair's or home," Josh finished.

Carrie spoke first, "Adair's would be fun, but Rory said he would host a post party. That would be more fun!" She looked around our circle of faces waiting for a reaction. Was this her way of saying she would rather be at the party with alcohol?

"I already told Rory we would go to his house," Matthew said, indicating this was not up for debate. Trisha seemed unalarmed by this news, so that plan must have already been established.

"Anna and I will probably stop by Adair's and

make a plan from there," Josh said then added, "We sat by Rory and Chloe at dinner earlier. He mentioned hosting, so we may end up there."

I could read through Josh's response and knew he had no intention of ending up at Rory's party. I didn't want to feel judged by these girls, however, so I added, "I didn't bring clothes to change into. Are you staying in your dresses?"

But no one answered because the slow song ended, and the volume went up as they announced the next song. We were suddenly swallowed by the throng moving closer to the center of the dance floor. Everyone was jumping in unison to the beat of the music.

With ringing ears and aching feet, we walked to the lobby of the Hilton an hour later. Josh put his tux coat on after digging out my cell phone and our valet ticket. We stopped at the desk to ask for the car and then found a sofa to rest on until the Corvette arrived.

"So, should we try Adair's party, or Rory's? Or I am completely fine if we just want to return Marcus's car and call it a night." Josh yawned and then laughed. "Dancing is exhausting."

The clock hanging above the valet's desk read quarter past midnight. I didn't have a curfew on Prom night, but I felt responsible for the car. Concluding that I wanted tonight to last just a little longer, I said, "Let's go to Adairs'. I do not want to go to Rory's. They've been drinking since dinner."

"Perfect," Josh said, and stood as the car pulled up to the curb. He stepped ahead of me and graciously opened my door. I threw my heels that I'd been carrying to the floor and slid into the seat.

I queued a song as we pulled away, but Josh immediately turned to volume down. "Traffic is going to be a nightmare getting out of here. I had at least ten notifications updating the score of the Cardinals game. They had an hour rain delay and it went into five extra innings, so they just finished playing."

"It's past midnight!" I exclaimed. "That's a late game!" As we drove west away from the Hilton I turned and looked back toward Busch Stadium. The lights still illuminated all of downtown St. Louis. Fans walking to their cars were scattered in all directions. We drove by a steel drum band on a sidewalk playing for tips. Despite the hour, I sensed excitement and knew the Cardinals were celebrating a victory.

We crawled through three blocks of dense traffic before we finally hit twenty miles per hour. Long streams of red and white reflected on the wet pavement from the traffic lights. Another red light caused Josh to brake suddenly, and we laughed as we jerked to an abrupt stop. "So sorry," Josh grinned, "I'll have to ask Marcus to borrow his car again so I can get used to the brakes." I looked past Josh to the car beside us, also stopped at the light. The passengers were an older couple, obvious Cardinal fans, and they were both laughing at us. They seemed to know we didn't belong in this fancy car, despite our formal attire.

I felt a vibration in my hand, heard the odd, but familiar sound of a text from my angel, and saw the traffic light turn green all in the same millisecond.

Don't go!

Stop!

Tell Josh to stop!

Her sudden and urgent plea gave me a heightened sense of awareness. The light was green. Josh was still smiling about giving us whiplash. His thigh was raising to move from the brake to the accelerator. I flashed my eyes to the intersection to find the danger she was trying to reveal. I heard the sweet notes of another angelic notification blaze through the ringing in my ears.

Noooo!

The headlights traveling south should have been slowing for their red light. My eyes could see through the beams to the filament within the bulb. The car was *not* slowing down.

Josh's foot pushed the gas pedal as my hand reached to simultaneously grab his arm. "STOP!" I screamed. His reflexes were too slow. His foot was still pushing the wrong pedal and we began moving forward into the path of the car that was still not braking for its red light. My intake of breath was so severe it hurt my throat. My brain registered this, however, and argued back that the pain of the collision would surpass the throat pain exponentially.

Josh's peripheral vision suddenly caught the moving light. His right hand flew from the steering wheel and using his arm, he shielded me. His foot slammed the brake as the airbags deployed. Hearing the horrific screeching of many vehicles braking and metal scraping with metal was surreal. The smell of the scene instantly filled my nostrils. The nylon airbag obstructed my view. Was Josh injured? Was our car damaged? How do I get away from this airbag? I felt a panic growing like flames inside my mind. It took maybe three seconds for these events to unfold. The sounds of my scream and the impact of cars colliding was instantly replaced with an eerie silence. I felt my own shallow breathing but felt disconnected from it.

"Anna?" Josh did not sound normal. "Anna, can you hear me?" Louder this time, but he still didn't sound like himself. My head pounded. The pain was trying to chisel its way out of my skull. "Anna, look at me," Josh pleaded.

My neck objected as I turned to face him. He looked normal. Thank God. He was okay, and maybe I was too. I should try talking. "Are you okay?" I whispered. "Did we hit that car that ran the red light?" I carefully lifted my hand to try to push back the slowly deflating airbag, but it was a wasted effort. It had me trapped. Luckily seeing Josh's face caused my panic to cool down a few degrees.

"How did you do it?" He asked, mystified. "How did you know I needed to stop?" Josh's eyes burned into mine and I was too scared to answer. I would never lie to Josh. But the truth? I would never tell him.

"I saw headlights," I managed to mumble. "I just thought they weren't going to stop." What if he heard my phone chime my angel's messages? Would he ask me about that too? Please someone get me out of this car, I wanted to scream!

We sat in silence for minutes, hours maybe, absorbing the shock. Sirens. There were sirens moving in our direction. I desperately needed out of this car. That odor intensified and plagued my senses. Outside in the intersection there was someone in greater need of attention than me. Someone was losing blood. I could smell it.

12 AFTER

"Oh, God," Josh cried when he finally climbed out of the car. My confusion was instantly combined with fear. Josh's tone indicated the scene hidden from my view was horrific. In seconds he was opening my door, offering me assistance. Not sure my limbs would function properly, and also hesitant to know what he knew, I clambered out, keeping my eyes down. Once vertical, I kept a tight grip on Josh's hand as he ushered me to move forward. Turning to face the intersection, I was bewildered.

The car with the Cardinal fans was still parallel to ours but shifted forward a few yards. The driver of the small truck that grazed the front of the Corvette and then hit the tail end of the car beside us, rested motionless over his steering wheel. He was wearing a tux jacket. Rory.

My mind and body felt as if they were under water. My senses betrayed me by working properly despite the weight pressing down on my thoughts. There were at least a dozen people trying to assist Rory and the couple in the car beside us. A few people were on their phones, hopefully requesting more help to arrive. Two ladies approached me asking something, but I couldn't hear their question with the ringing in my ears. They seemed desperate to help me, but I couldn't form a sentence. Josh released my hand and spoke to them urgently. The two strangers escorted me to a sidewalk nearby and sat with me while we watched. Josh ran to Rory's truck, but did not open the door. Drawing both hands to his own head he called out in agony, "Rory!" As I pieced together each scene playing in front of me, I did my best to pull myself from the drowning sensation.

I watched helplessly as two ambulances finally arrived. Paramedics ran to both Rory's truck and the car with the Cardinal fans. They worked quickly assessing and stabilizing the injured. Josh had taken several steps back but stayed close enough to observe Rory's condition. I wanted to sprint to his side. Choosing to stay with my strangers, I sent a silent prayer to my angel.

A uniformed officer knelt in front of me asking calmly, "Ma'am, do you want a blanket? You look cold and uncomfortable sitting here in a dress and no shoes." I glanced at my feet. I hadn't even realized I was barefoot.

Mustering the strength to answer him, I looked at the ladies at my sides for support. "My shoes are in that car," I said, pointing to Marcus's Corvette.

No longer barefoot, I sat in an uncomfortable waiting room chair staring at a hospital clock. Black frame, white face, black numbers. Black stick hands told me it was three eighteen in the morning. I thought about its ticking and forced myself *not* to think about batteries. My dad met us at the hospital over an hour ago with clothes for Josh and me to change into. He sat next to me, mindlessly scrolling through his phone. Josh sat across from me. He was busy on his phone, too. He had been texting for most of an hour trying to figure out why Chloe wasn't in Rory's truck. He finally heard back from Carrie that Chloe had been found passed out in the restroom at the Hilton. Her parents had been notified, and they had left the dance shortly after midnight. Syd and Marcus came to the hospital, but after being reassured Josh and I were unharmed, left. They had a long day ahead figuring out insurance and getting Marcus's car repaired. Luckily, the damage was minimal compared to Rory's truck and the second car he hit. I told them to keep my Jeep. It would be awhile before I would be willing to drive. Simply getting into my Dad's car to get to the hospital seemed taxing.

Rory's parents both impatiently paced the hallway between the waiting room and the nurses' station. At exactly three twenty-four a blonde nurse bounded through the doors separating us from Rory. "Mr. and Mrs. Ransdell?" She smiled brightly, despite the hour. Nurses who work night shifts amazed me. Her blue eyes were shining with friendliness. "My name is Rachel. Dr. Parks was called back to the ER, so he told me to relay his report on Rory." She reached out and put her hand on Mrs. Ransdell's shoulder. "Rory is going to make a complete recovery," Rachel said. "His head took a pretty hard hit, but was unconscious for such a short period, he only displayed two markers of a concussion. He has nineteen stitches in his forehead, but otherwise is very healthy and uninjured. Mostly just bruised and sore." Her report brought tears to both of Rory's parents. Mrs.

Ransdell even hugged Rachel.

"Thank you," Mr. Ransdell replied, choked up, but obviously relieved. "Will we be able to talk to Dr. Parks anytime tonight, or I guess I mean this morning?"

Rachel glanced back toward the doors where she had entered the waiting room. "That I'm not sure. I will let the next attendant know you wish to speak to a doctor, and we'll see what we can do." She smiled one last time before turning to walk back to the nurses' station, and added, "Rory is one lucky kid! He must have someone pretty special watching over him to walk away with just a bump on his head and a few stitches."

I had been listening intently to what the nurse was reporting to the Ransdells. Relief washed over me as soon as she mentioned Rory being healthy and uninjured. Our prayers had been answered. Not only were Josh, Rory, and I mostly unscathed, the passengers of the third car also miraculously walked away with only minor injuries. The nurse said someone special was watching over Rory. Was she referring to my angel? Was that even possible? The heaviness of the night seemed to lighten dramatically. I reached for my phone that I had tucked away earlier. Would there be a message from Mom? She helped all of us escape from what could have been another tragedy. My mind was reeling until I swiped my phone on and discovered no new notifications.

"Expecting a call?" My Dad looked at my phone, and then into my eyes, puzzled.

"I just...I...I thought I heard a text," I lied.

Shoving it back in my bag, I stood and walked to Rory's parents. Dad and Josh followed. "That's great news!" I exclaimed, "Just what we were hoping to hear." I hugged Mrs. Ransdell even though we'd only been introduced a couple hours ago. She smiled and hugged me back, wiping away a new wave of tears.

My Dad spoke to Mr. Ransdell quietly while Josh also offered Rory's Mom a hug and more words of encouragement. We said our goodbyes to the Ransdells, promising to be of any help and hoping to stay informed on Rory's release.

"Rory is lucky. There's no doubt about that," my Dad said as we got on the elevator taking us to the parking garage. "He's in for a world of hurt when he finds out he still has to face prosecution for driving under the influence, and his traffic violations. He'll probably have to pay thousands and possibly serve time. Nothing good ever comes from a night of drinking." Dad stared at the elevator doors closing and said nothing more, seemingly lost in thought. His statement gave me hope that he was referring to his own drinking as well. My own thoughts were transitioning to a desire to sleep. Tonight's events had me feeling wired, but sleep would soon overtake my wakefulness.

After showering, I crawled into bed at almost five in the morning. Thank goodness there was no need to set an alarm. My eyes were closed before I even made myself comfortable, hoping sleep would come fast.

Sweet dreams, my love.

My Mom's text was the comfort I needed to extinguish the flame of this lengthy day. Typing my reply was difficult, exhaustion made my vision blurry.

Thank you for helping us!

I wasn't expecting another message, or maybe my brain was too tired to process if I even looked at my phone again. Maybe it was just a dream, but I thought I heard her actual voice reply, *I will always be near.*

After Prom, the drama of the collision, and Rory finally returning to school, the remainder of the school year seemed quite anticlimactic. Rory was placed on probation, was expected to complete five hundred hours of community service and lost his license for two years. Our last week of school lunch periods were spent coming up with creative things Rory could do to fill the service hours. Josh had the best idea when he suggested that Rory should volunteer to clean at the Butterfly House. The only obstacles separating us from graduation were finals. I discovered that finals were manageable. Considering the events, I had already survived the last eight months, taking a few tests caused little stress.

I had not put much thought into celebrating graduation until the week of the ceremonies. I had ordered announcements back in February, but they were never addressed. The boxes of stationery sat unopened on my closet floor. I was taken by surprise one evening when Josh called my Dad's phone. The two of us were sitting at the kitchen table finishing our Thai take out when his phone rang. Listening to Dad's side of the conversation, however, gave me enough clues to figure out the Cabels were invited to the Justice graduation festivities. "Tell your parents thank you in advance and let me know if there is any other way we can contribute. I know this will please Anna, and of course Syd and me as well. Thanks again." Dad ended the call and turned to me with a hopeful expression. "The Justice family would like us to come to their farm Saturday evening for a picnic style graduation party. Josh said casual."

I smiled broadly, picturing Josh rehearsing the conversation and dialing my Dad's number. "That was kind of him to call you. Honestly, it makes me a little nervous. He didn't mention anything to me about having a party together," I said, my curiosity growing. Cheyenne was stationed at my feet and I looked to her for advice. "Chey, do you want to go to a party at Josh's?" I grinned and offered her my last bite of chicken.

"I think his parents want to provide you with an enjoyable end to your high school career, without making us feel like a charity case," Dad chuckled at this. "I'm guessing they assumed I had made no plans to celebrate my favorite girl." Dad cleared our paper boxes and plastic utensils, throwing everything away, leaving no evidence of the feast we just devoured. I got up to find a cloth and made myself busy wiping the table. I liked this time I had with my father, and I knew these quick meals and conversations were numbered. In just a couple months I would be packing and moving out.

"Do you want some brownies?" I asked, trying to

postpone both of us retiring for the evening. Making dessert would surely prolong our conversation. I found a mix in the pantry and started the process before he answered.

"I didn't save room for brownies, but that never stopped me before," Dad finally replied. He was browsing his phone, focused on something.

"Are we responsible for providing anything for the picnic Saturday?" I was hoping Syd would have an opportunity to provide an amazing dish. I would be proud to arrive with one of his beautiful sugary masterpieces. A definite contrast to my brownies from a box. I turned from my stirring and looked back at my dad who was still staring at his phone, "Dad?"

"Sorry." He turned his phone off and placed it face down on the table. "What did you ask me?"

"Never mind," I said. I could ask Josh about what we needed to bring. And I dared not ask Dad what he was searching on his phone. He likely just realized he might want to get me a graduation gift. While this might hurt someone else's feelings, it left me worried one more time about how Dad would take care of himself and his responsibilities when I left for college.

Luckily, before my thoughts could sink too low, Syd bounded through the door from the garage. He was beaming, and it was obvious he had news to share.

Syd set down two grocery bags on the counter and promptly circled around to face us. "Go ahead...Ask me!" He was clearly about to burst. He sat down with Dad at the table then immediately popped up and walked a lap around the kitchen.

I abandoned the brownie mix and sat down at the table again. Dad wore Syd's matching smile. "Spill it," he said, amusement in his voice.

"You know how Marcus took a new job at that startup company in Chesterfield? So, they're designing an app to run much like a magazine, but obviously digital because no one knows how to turn pages anymore." At this Syd continued with huge gestures as he paced the kitchen. "Well Marcus was bragging to his little team about my culinary skills and then begged me to bring in my breakfast souffles last week, which I did, because I'm nice, and I admit, I like showing off." He moved to his bags of groceries and started unpacking their contents. As he talked, he organized the food by the sink. "Well, little did I know that this digital magazine was planning to feature not only local hot spots, but also local talent!" Syd stopped arranging food and looked at us. "I am going to be the first face of Arch! They want to feature me prepping a garden party! They want to launch it in two weeks!" Syd laughed at himself and added, "Remind me to stop teasing Marcus about this being a bragazine."

I got up to hug my amazing uncle. "I'm so proud of you! You will do great. I wish I could help somehow, it sounds like a huge undertaking." I silently wished my boxed brownies weren't sitting on the counter. "Do you know what you'll prepare?"

"No. Not at all. I am sure they have a layout

already in production. I'm probably expected to provide photos and recipes to fill the holes." Syd's adorable face was lit with an expression of glee.

My mind darted back to the graduation picnic we were invited to. "Well here's some news that lends itself to your new endeavor." I took a dramatic pause waiting for Syd to focus less on his groceries and become more curious of my announcement. Taking my bait, he turned and looked, waiting for me to finish. "The Justice family invited the three of us, and Marcus too if he's available, to a graduation picnic on Saturday. It would only be polite if we offered to contribute to the meal." I waved my hand toward the forgotten brownies on the counter. "I hardly think my skills are worthy. How about you practice for your garden party by making something for us to take?" I smiled and batted my eyelashes a couple of times just to make Syd laugh.

Syd froze on the spot and said nothing. He was obviously processing this information because he kept a smile on his face. He finally responded but spoke quickly, his excitement reigniting, "Wait. Where's the picnic?" He pulled his phone out of his jacket pocket and started scrolling. "This Saturday Marcus and I had plans that can easily be rearranged." He made some swipes on his phone and typed something in without losing his constant grin. "There. Done. Just cleared my calendar. You didn't answer. Where is this gathering?"

Syd's eagerness for information was promising. He was definitely interested in helping the Justice family. "It's at their farm. They called it a picnic, so I assume it will be near the barn where they have a flat grassy spot with a few tables" I did my best to describe the setting then added, "it's surrounded by trees, so It has lots of shade."

I looked to Dad, hoping for his input. "If Josh said the picnic was casual, don't you think they would appreciate the help? It would be a perfect opportunity for Syd to have a run through of his garden party?"

Dad laughed at my question. "You sound like you're selling a car. But you make a good sale. I'm sure they'd love the help with food." He picked up his phone and started texting. "The only way we can know for sure is to ask." Dad finished typing his message and stared at his screen as if it would just spit the answer, but of course he had to wait for Josh's reply.

I returned to my brownies. They needed to be out of Syd's workspace and in the oven. They weren't gourmet, but they would still taste good. Pouring them into a pan and shoving them into the preheated oven, I set a timer and returned to the table with dad.

Josh's reply pinged on my Dad's phone and he read it aloud. "Mom says she would love Syd's expert help. She is out of town until Thursday so planning the picnic was going to be rushed anyway! Can I send Syd her contact info so they can plan?" Dad set his phone down and looked at Syd. "I think you're hired!"

13 SUMMER

Saturday's forecast was cooperating nicely for outdoor activities. I woke early and took Cheyenne for a walk in our neighborhood. Normally dad walked Chey, but he mentioned the night before that he needed to work until noon. The house was quiet when I browsed around the kitchen looking for breakfast. Syd must be at the market buying the fresh foods for tonight's party. Cheyenne followed me around the kitchen hoping I would share something other than dry dog food. I made peanut butter toast for myself and offered her a giant scoop of peanut butter. As she licked the spoon, I held out to her we had a good chat.

"Now you do realize I will be moving soon, right?" She stared at me while her tongue made happy swipes at the peanut butter. "Don't be worried about me meeting any other puppies, there won't be any of those where I'm going. And you better still love me the most when I come home, which will be often. Because I will miss your furry face. And dad. And Josh. And Syd." This one-sided conversation was borderline comical, so I kept all sadness out of my voice. When I pulled the spoon away, Cheyenne flopped down, her paws covering my feet protectively. I felt loved. "Make sure to take dad for long walks. It's good therapy, you know." I rubbed her head gently until she seemed drowsy enough for me to extract my feet. "Good talk, girl," I whispered and tiptoed upstairs to shower and spend extra time prepping and pampering before the events began. Josh and I had planned a lunch date and an afternoon together at the Missouri Botanical Garden. He promised I would be impressed with its eighty acres of beauty. I was guessing it was more than just neat rows of flowers. Especially since he said the food was amazing, and there was often live music. I changed clothes several times before settling on an ivory sweater over a favorite old tee shirt and jeans. I was slipping on my Vans when a text dinged my phone.

Be there in fifteen! Ready?

Was I surprised Josh was early? Definitely not. I pulled my hair into a tight ponytail, hoping it would be manageable later for the party. I replied back to Josh and sent my Dad a quick text reminding him I would be out all afternoon. One last check in the mirror and I was ready. I grinned at my reflection momentarily to see if it matched my mood. It seemed to coordinate. The new camera was securely packed in a shoulder bag I found in the back of my closet. Adjusting the bag to fit comfortably, I reached for my phone resting on my dresser as I exited my bedroom. A text banner illuminated the screen. I hadn't heard a text arrive. But it was clearly there, and it was from my angel.

When you smile it is contagious.

How odd. She had not sent me a message since the night of Prom several weeks ago. Suddenly, my date with Josh seemed insignificant. A desire crept over me to sit and talk to her. I longed for the conversations we shared and her loving wisdom, expressed more in listening than a disquisition. She typically let me figure things out on my own.

I've tried my hardest to experience senior year, but now I'm glad its over and can celebrate surviving it. Wish you could celebrate with us too.

I set my bag down in the hallway and leaned on the wall waiting for her reply.

I admire your positive attitude. It will help you survive the greatest of obstacles. Go relish this day!

As always, she was still helping, advising, and loving. I smiled at my screen, and then read her final text...

See, it's contagious :)

I retrieved my bag and slid my phone in its front pocket. The doorbell rang twice, announcing Josh's eagerness to explore a new locale. I descended the stairs two at a time. Swinging the door open, I wanted to experiment with my contagious smile, but Josh wore one brighter than mine.

"Hi!" he blurted. Stepping away from the house, he extended his arm as an invitation to lead him back out to his truck. "You look adorable," he added, slightly less breathless.

"Are you ok?" I questioned, although gauging from his expression, it wasn't a matter of if he was ok, but more what was he hiding?

"Of course!" he exclaimed in a higher voice than normal. "Just…let's go…I mean, here we go!"

"You're a horrible liar," I scolded, hearing the humor in my own voice. "And I despise surprises, so spill it." I led Josh to the door of his truck with exaggerated stomps and yanked the handle. I guess I didn't *really* hate surprises, flashing back to Cheyenne and Alexandra's driveway arrivals. I could see in the window of the cab and knew nothing was waiting on the seat for me this time. But I was wrong. Opening the door revealed a bouquet of fresh cut long stem white roses.

Josh caught my shoulder and turned me around before I could reach for the flowers. "Today is all about you and me." His smile never fading, he continued, "My parents are so excited to host the party tonight, we have all day to celebrate graduation and…" he trailed off. He pulled me into a tight embrace but let go before I could reciprocate. Lifting the plastic wrapped bundle and placing them in my arms, he finished, "These are for you, but I was hoping before we went to the gardens you would introduce me to your Mom. You can share your roses with her?" He looked into my eyes and I wondered if he could read my thoughts. Behind my smiling eyes there was a jumble of joy and grief, mixed with some kind of admiration.

"I was just thinking about my Mom a few minutes ago. Before you arrived." I hoped I sounded truthful. I *was* thinking about her as we shared that short text exchange. What an amazing person he was, thinking past me, and offering such a gift. Josh's smile never wavered. His confidence added to the kind gesture. It gave me confidence, it too was contagious, I guess.

Shifting the flowers, I wrapped my free arm around Josh's waist and felt him hug me properly. "My Mom already loves you, but yes, let's deliver some beautiful roses."

Our drive to the cemetery was contradictory of how any human would normally approach a loved one's grave. We bellowed classic rock hits and joked about Cheyenne graduating obedience school and her future aspirations.

I pulled one stem to save for myself and handed Josh the remaining roses. "These are from you, so you can properly introduce yourself," I giggled.

"I'm glad you agreed to this, Anna," his warm smile felt better than the sun cascading through the trees full of new spring leaves. A calm sensation washed over me, replacing the peculiar giddiness I was experiencing. The quiet cemetery that so often filled my heart with dread, was comforting at this moment.

"Let's go meet Eleanora Cabel," I beamed, linking my arm through his.

When we returned to the truck a short time later there was another text waiting for me.

Thank you for the roses. He's a keeper ;)

****

Finally removing my sandals from my complaining feet, I threw them toward the stairs. Not even taking time to find a good show, I simply turned the tv on to whatever channel the last viewer had abandoned. I wanted some background noise but was not interested in watching. I made myself comfortable on the couch with a blanket and my phone. I couldn't wait to tell Alexandra about my day and ask about hers. Coincidentally, her graduation party had also been scheduled for today. I guessed she would have beat me home, even with our time difference. Her celebration was planned for brunch and extending to a late lunch. I started our conversation by sending a photo of Syd and me posing by his exquisite spread. It was an extraordinary gift that he could make food look like art. Along with the photo I added,

We ate like champs thanks to syd! How was your party? Congrats by the way…we graduated!

While waiting for Alex's reply, I scrolled through my Instagram feed. Josh and Syd had both just posted photos of our evening together. Syd's humility shined as his images were only of guests. He was obviously going to let someone else share his hard work. Syd had posted a really nice one of my dad laughing and another of me sitting with Josh. It must have been taken when we were talking about my graduation ceremony near mishap when I practically fell into Principal Justice as he handed me a diploma. I looked embarrassed in the photo. I giggled at the memory and took a screenshot of both. Josh posted a single snapshot of me hugging his Mom before we left. I took a screenshot of this one as well. His caption was potent.

My girls.

14 GOODBYE

Ice cream?

Josh's text was the distraction I needed from packing. I had been in my room cleaning, organizing, and reminiscing for over three hours. Only one of the three boxes intended for the clothes needed for my first semester of college was full. Too easily sidetracked, I feared it would take me every minute of my last two days in St. Louis to finish packing.

Yes, please! Ted Drewes? I need a break. Can we go soon?

I hastily changed into nicer shorts, a soft violet sleeveless blouse, and slid into my favorite sandals before exiting my room. I felt irresponsible abandoning the empty boxes, but I needed to spend time with Josh. He had texted back.

Absolutely! Be there soon.

Searching the house for Dad or Syd, I located them both, along with Marcus and Cheyenne, sitting on the back patio. All three were laughing uncontrollably as I stepped outside. Seeing their smiles brightened the already sun filled summer afternoon. "What's up?" I questioned, taking the last seat at the table. Cheyenne left her post by dad and sat beside me. My hand automatically started rubbing her ears.

"Well, your uncle was approached by a female today," Dad responded, laughter still coating his words.

"Oh yeah, how'd that go?" I inquired with a matching smile.

Syd leaned forward and cleared his throat. "I was my usual charming self and went along with all her flirtatious comments. I didn't lead her to believe I was interested, nor did I insinuate I was seeing someone."

Marcus piped up, holding back more laughter, "We were at the farmers' market, and I didn't know what I was interrupting when I walked up behind Syd and wrapped my arms around him in an embrace that quite literally took that girl's breath away. She choked out a couple words, turned a lovely shade of crimson, and fled."

"You have a different affect on the ladies, Marcus. I draw them in, you scare them away," Syd chortled playfully.

"Unfortunately, I'm guessing I scared her away from the market as well," Marcus added boastfully.

Syd stared at me momentarily then asked, "You're looking especially radiant. Are you going somewhere?"

"I guess that's the end of that conversation," Marcus chided, rolling his eyes at Syd.

"Josh is rescuing me from the disaster of my room. Packing is complicated. How am I supposed to know what I need? There's not enough space in our dorm for everything I want to take," I said. "I guess it gives me an excuse to come back if I'm missing something important."

Dad responded with amazement in his tone, "You're planning on returning? I imagined you'd be living your best life and forget about us fellas." He reached for my hand and gave it a squeeze.

"You're not serious, are you?" I said. He surely knew I was hesitant about being away from my family. Thinking back through our conversations from the past couple of months I could not recall ever showing excitement about moving. "My friends are counting down until they leave for college. I've been counting the days I have left with you guys." Tension crept into my shoulders knowing I had abruptly ended their humorous conversation.

Syd sensed this and spoke up, "Anna, you're going to love college. And we know you'll be home as often as you see fit."

"Sorry, I did not mean to make you feel like you were abandoning us," Dad added. "It will be an adjustment, but we're happy for you to experience independence."

I moved around the table and initiated a hug with Dad and then Syd. Marcus must have felt left out because he too stood, anticipating a hug. "I've never been to Lawrence, so you can expect us to make a trip or two there to see you as well."

"That would be great, Marcus! Maybe you guys can visit when Alexandra's family is in Kansas so we're all together. You'd love her family." I felt my phone vibrate and checked the screen.

I'm here. Want me to come in?

Knowing if Josh came in, we'd be obligated to stay and talk for I while, so I used this as my ticket out.

I will be right out!

"Josh is here. Is it okay if we go get ice cream? I probably won't want dinner later if I eat a concrete," I hedged, not wanting to disappoint them if they were making a plan for dinner.

"What do you mean, *concrete*?" My dad asked, completely intrigued.

Syd laughed, "You've never been to Ted Drewes?" He elbowed Marcus. "I vote concrete for dinner too! We'll explain to Christopher the other world of concrete, Anna. You two go enjoy the afternoon!"

Climbing into Josh's truck ushered another wave of emotions. How long would it be until I rode with him again? Would he invite a new girl to sit here?

"You look puzzled. What are you thinking about?" Josh misses nothing.

Will you find a new girlfriend? "I was thinking about being picked up in your pickup," I lied. "I will miss this," I clarified.

Josh pulled away from the curb smiling. "Same here, but we're not talking about leaving, or college, or anything like that today. Today we're getting ice cream, and I have one more St. Louis field trip for you. Just to rub it in a little how magnificent our city is." He took his eyes off the road to glance at me, still grinning. "If you're still in love with St. Louis then I know I have a chance for you to always return, to me." He reached for his stereo and turned up the volume and began singing along to Toto's *Africa*. I joined the chorus and let myself enjoy the present, giving tomorrow and the future no more thought.

We took our time at Ted Drewes, thinking my dad, Syd, and Marcus might show up. I took a picture of my concrete and sent it to dad.

Turtle is my favorite at TDs. Are you coming?

"Thank you for letting me have a turn paying for this," I said to Josh, holding up my ice cream.

"Thank you for treating me. I'm confident I will be able to return the favor. We will have to research local favorites in Columbia and Lawrence." Josh stirred his cup absentmindedly as he spoke.

"I thought we weren't talking about college today," I teased. Watching him carefully, not sure what I was hoping to read from him.

"We're talking about ice cream, not college. I think it is important for us to test ice cream, preferably this custard type, and share with each other our findings."

"So, when I find the very best custard in Lawrence you'll drive there just to verify?" I asked, playing along with this scenario.

"Absolutely, and likewise. You'll come to Columbia to help me decide on a favorite. This is important data that will contribute to a successful college career." Josh took his last bite and tossed his cup in the trash. Facing me again he continued, "I'll pay next time."

"Sounds like a plan," I giggled. "You know I won't ever turn down ice cream."

"That's the beautiful thing about us. We are both willing to sacrifice time and gas money for the greater good. For the love of ice cream."

His simple words were the confirmation I needed to hear. I smiled and took a selfie of Josh, myself, and my ice cream. A promise made.

"Is your family coming?" Josh asked. "Because we need to be moving on." He looked at his phone for the time. "City Garden closes soon."

"City Garden?" I had never heard of it. Memories of City Museum swept my mind, curious if it would be as obscure.

"Let's go check it out," Josh reached for my hand

and held it as we walked to his truck. I sent dad a text with my free hand.

Enjoy the custard! We are going to city garden.

I overslept the next morning. Normally, this would cause irritation, but instead, I stayed in bed trying hard to reinvent the dream that hadn't quite faded. The familiar scene of a colorful lake surrounded by lush trees was intact. Someone had been sitting with me. But who? Wakefulness was overtaking sleep. As the images blurred to nothing, I allowed myself to open my eyes. Knowing I wouldn't be able to sleep late again for days, I began checking social media and looking at pictures from City Garden. The time spent with Josh was no disappointment. The flowers and fountains were remarkable. It was fun to wind around, exploring with Josh. Our conversation was light and full of laughter, never returning to the topics of college, leaving, or ice cream dates. My full body jolted under my blanket when a text banner appeared, covering a photo I had taken of Josh by a statue.

Good morning, Tiddlywinks!

It had been countless days since her last message illuminated my screen.

Hi was all I could manage to respond. How I wished her voice was in my room to wake me, talk to me, and help me through my last days in this house.

Finished packing yet?

She knew what was on my heart. I did not have her voice, but I had her encouragement. How could I encompass all the fears and questions into one text?

I have to finish today. Tomorrow is moving day. It's overwhelming.

I adjusted my pillows and blanket, so I was seated upright for this conversation. Imagining my mom sitting on the edge of the bed, I waited for her reply. No words came, so I typed again.

Knowing I can return from ku anytime is reassuring, but it doesn't take away the dreadful feeling of leaving dad.

This time her reply was immediate.

Your dad's depression has been crippling. That is a normal response to loss. He is ready to live again, Anna.

I read her message twice but could think of no words to agree or disagree with her statement. How was she so confident?

It is time for you to live too. You are surrounded by people who love and support you. Even if you're miles or memories away. Go.

Her unspoken words were as powerful as they were made possible. I could go. Dad would be fine. Not easy, or perfect, but possible.

Thank you. I miss having you close.

I felt tears forming as I read her next message.

You have me for eternity. Enjoy your years. It's only a blink of what you really have left.

Her words resonated through my mind. This was her goodbye. I was frozen, just staring at the text. The finality was trickling from my mind to my limbs, causing a numb sensation. She had once said she would be here as long as I needed help.

See you again.

My final reply. Three words I hoped she would hold until the moment I would see her glorious face. It was obvious this farewell would fare lighter than the grief stricken one back in October. Maybe this goodbye I would store in my heart, rather than my feet.

The final task to check off the list before my departure was complete. The empty frames of the locket my Dad gave me on Christmas were full. Knowing I could text Dad and Josh at any given moment and they would instantly reply meant they were still close. Thanks to technology, instant communication made home feel tangible. But there were two loves that I could not text or communicate with in any way, anymore. Mom and Cheyenne. So, their tiny faces would live in my locket, hanging close to my heart today, and forever.

Dad's suburban was overflowing with my bags of

clothes, bedding, and the few mementos I wanted in the dorm I was sharing with Alexandra. Cheyenne was safely harnessed in the front passenger seat of my Jeep. Her kennel was folded neatly in the back seat for her return home to Missouri after my Kansas drop off. Syd and Marcus joined our entourage, demanding they were entitled to this send off party. I didn't argue of course. I wanted a few more hours together before the rest of my life began. Wishing Josh would come too, I was disappointed, but understanding of his new schedule, new home, new life. I was confident he would text or call me daily.

Dad appeared at the driver's side window. His smile was bright, but his eyes seemed wary. "Are you sure you don't want me to drive with you? Syd could pilot the suburban." My need to make this trip solo overpowered the sadness of moving away from my father.

"I think I should drive myself, Dad. You know, get used to the route." A shard of guilt punctured my heart as I added, "Can you use the driving time to make some work calls?"

He smirked, knowing I was using his cell phone use as an excuse. "Sure, I actually do need to make some calls regarding the wind farm project. There's a bit of a hiccup in progress. The roads they built for our mixer trucks aren't adequate." He walked around the front of the Jeep and opened Cheyenne's passenger door. I had already secured her harness, but it was reassuring to have Dad double check. "We'll be close to the wind farm. It's just an hour north of I-70. We could extend our day by driving up there?" He said this with such sincerity I believed his suggestion. Then a wide grin broke his determined stare. "I'm just kidding! We don't have time for that today. But you are closer to the turbines than we are here in St. Louis, so I'd imagine you'll visit soon." He winked and ended our conversation, "You lead the way. I love you, Anna."

"Love you, too, Dad," I whispered. I stared at Cheyenne after Dad shut the passenger door and walked to the suburban. "It's fine, Chey. Dad likes driving by himself and I have you to keep me company. I'm sure he'll break his own rule and text me every fifteen minutes while we're on the road."

A smack on my window made me jump and let out an audible squeak. "Syd!" I laughed in embarrassment and lowered my window. "Don't do that!"

"Sorry, Love, just wanted to say bye to your beautiful face," he offered as he tried hugging me through the small space of the open window. "I'm saving my warm and benevolent farewell for later this evening. So, for now, don't drive like an old lady." He kissed my cheek and turned to walk to his car parked by the curb.

I called to his retreating back, "I love you, Syd!"

Syd looked back to me with his genuine toothy smile, "I know. Love you, too, and I'm always near. Always."

Cheyenne barked, interrupting my thoughts. I

think she sensed the shift in my emotions. "I wuff you, too, girl. Let's go before I change my mind."

I searched my phone for an appropriate departure tune. I had a four-hour playlist prepared. Plenty of upbeat songs to keep me awake and distracted for the long drive to Kansas. Cheyenne would be good company, but not much of a conversationalist. I added one more song thinking it was perfect for pulling away from my St. Louis home. My short time in Missouri was filled with extreme emotions and experiences. The death of my Mother, and the beginning of a few new lifelong relationships. Or at least I'd like to think of Josh and Cheyenne as lifelong companions. I tapped play on my phone, turned up the volume of Tonight Alive's *Oxygen*, and drove away from the curb.

Dear Reader,

Please let me share my gratitude for being loyal to Anna and her family. Reading the entirety of this story hopefully left you feeling not only saddened by the grief of Anna's circumstances, but humored as well. Despite his grieving, Christopher was able to provide Anna with unconditional love. Syd never failed at trying to lift everyone's mood with his quirkiness. I found Josh, as well, to be comforting with his constant friendship that developed into love. Anna was lucky to be surrounded by characters who not only supported her, but also adored her. She reciprocated their love and will likely grow in her faith and mature into a loving wife and mother.

And speaking of Anna's future, now you are in control. In the hundreds of stories, I have read in my lifetime, I am forever wishing the endings were slightly different than how the authors chose to disembark their works. I always want to read more, know more, but the authors just let their ships sail. So now *you* have the opportunity to finish Anna's story.

Anna's future has endless possibilities as she leaves for college. Will she stay all four years in Kansas, graduate early, or transfer during her college career? Will she return to Missouri to be close to her father and Josh, or find a career Wyoming, the home she misses? Will her relationship with Josh thrive, ending in marriage, or will she find another love? I would like to think she enjoys a life of happiness and the love she deserves after suffering such pain as a teenager, but we all know life is full of surprises and multiple heartbreaks. Do not forget about Christopher. Will his grieving heart be open to welcome companionship, or will he be a perpetual bachelor? Syd and Marcus are a fun pair, what do they have to look forward to? And furry Cheyenne, I hope she has a special place in your ending. So, what do their futures hold? You're sailing this ship now.

Love, Jill

ACKNOWLEDGEMENT

A very special thank you to my editing team. Jason, without you, this book would still be a document on my laptop. Carole & Tim Pilkington, your knowledge and heart-felt input gave me the confidence to move forward.

I would like to express gratitude to my family and friends who were an influence on the characters in my story.

Love to all who have read the book.